DREAM
HORSE

DREAM HORSE

Mary Sharp

*Allen Junior
Fiction*

Published in Great Britain in 1991 by
J A Allen & Co. Ltd.
1 Lower Grosvenor Place
London SW1W OEL
© Mary Sharp, 1991

ISBN 0−85131−531−3

British Library Cataloguing in Publication Data
Sharp, Mary
    Dream horse.
    I. Title
    823.914 [J]

ISBN 0−85131−531−3

Dedication

For Suzanne and Richard and Julia

CONTENTS

ONE
Easter holidays at last

I opened my eyes, shut them again quickly, and rolled over, remembering. I'd had a brilliant dream — another one about the black stallion, swimming with me in the sea. I'd dreamed about him before; it was magic while it lasted, pure magic.

Magic! That sounded right; that's what I'd call him. Black Magic: a good name for a black stallion.

The tide was high. I could hear it slapping against the stone quay wall outside my window. Perhaps that was why I had dreamed about waves and water. But why did I dream so often of the black horse? I couldn't understand why he was so real to me, why I could feel and touch him, and even when I woke I could still smell the damp horse scent and hear the sound of his breathing as he carried me on his back in the breaking waves.

I hadn't been afraid, just excited, and I wished passionately as I lay in bed that it could come true. Perhaps it was a good omen that I kept having the same dream, but I doubted it. It would never happen.

I closed my eyes tighter, trying to recapture the images of the shining horse and the white tumbling water, but it was no use; they had faded as dreams do, leaving me disappointed again.

It was time to get up. At any minute the alarm would ring in my ear. Then, with a great sigh of relief, I realised — Easter! Easter already, and the first morning of the holidays. Two weeks of holidays. It was bliss to think that I could lie in bed instead of dragging myself out at seven to get ready for school. No walking up the hill before I was properly awake, no shivering on the cold draughty corner waiting for the school bus to rumble round, like some unwelcome monster coming to swallow me up and take me away, when all I wanted to do was to stay at home.

I burrowed down sleepily again, pulling the covers over my head to shut out the light. But sleep was a long way off.

"Becky, Becky, wake up, it's Easter." It was my younger sister Joanna, from the other bed.

I sighed. "I know it's Easter, but I don't have to get up — not at crack of dawn. Go to sleep again."

"I can't. I've been awake for ages, listening to

you snoring."

"I don't snore. I was dreaming."

"What about? You did sound funny."

I didn't reply. I wasn't going to explain to a five-year-old about the black stallion. I hoped she'd leave me alone, but she didn't. Now she'd woken her Jack Russell, Brock, who had been curled on her feet. He bounded up on to my bed to lick my face, and I gave up trying to sleep.

Joanna was up now, and climbing on my bed, rolling the little rough-haired dog over and over, making him snap.

"Do you think we'll be allowed our Easter eggs today?" she asked me.

"Of course not," I replied crossly. "You know we never have them until Sunday. Now go away and be quiet. Go away," I repeated, pushing the dog away. "I've only got two weeks to stay in bed late — I'm staying put for another ten minutes. And take that animal with you."

"All right then. I'll go in to Jon and see if he's awake."

She pattered out noisily, followed by Brock, and I heard a disgruntled grumbling and a banging door from the next bedroom, followed by a shout of "you pig!" from Joanna. The day had started for those two as it usually did.

Our brother Jonathan was ten, and still at the village school. He couldn't wait to leave. He said it was boring. Perhaps it was, but I remembered how I'd cried the day I'd left. But then I'd cried the day I first went there as well. Never again, though, until the day I had to say goodbye to the two old classrooms and concrete playground that were as familiar to me as my own house and garden. Soon it would be Jonathan's turn to mix with more than eight hundred other children; I wondered what he'd make of it.

I hated the bus ride to the comprehensive school, squashed three in a seat designed for two, swaying and bumping along the narrow lanes, and tearing at frightening speed down the steep hills. Twelve tedious and time-wasting miles, although the school was only three miles away down the river.

Inside the bus you could hardly hear yourself think, for the noise of shouting from one end of the bus to the other. Any talk you could understand was about pop music, clothes, pubs, or boys (or girls). No-one talked about horses. Everyone seemed to be eating all the time; crisps, chocolate, chewing gum. Or drinking cans of coke or lager and lime, and throwing the empties out of the bus window along with the crisp packets.

The first-years had to steer clear of the older ones, otherwise we were likely to get our bags nicked and emptied all over the bus floor, or our homework held fluttering out of the window. The journey was always a nightmare; all I wanted was to be at home, in the fields or woods with the dog, or on the river or at the beach.

I lay staring at the ceiling and the globe of the paper lampshade, which was blue with white cloud shapes. Outside, the last of the March winds were blowing down the river, just outside my window. I could sense the chill in the air, even from the warmth of the bed. March had been wet and stormy, cold and inhospitable. The pathway to the house through the woods, next to the river bank, was treacherous with black and muddy leafmould, decaying and slippery; the garden was uninviting, the sands in the river where you could walk at low water clammy and cold.

I didn't go there so often now, since my adventure at Christmas, when the bait-digger had rescued me just in time from the quicksands.

I got up quickly, to stop myself thinking about it, making plans in my head for the holidays. The only blot on the horizon was the sponsored fast that the school had arranged, beginning on Easter Saturday. We had to fast for twenty-four hours, in aid of starving people in Ethiopia. It hadn't sounded too bad when I'd agreed to do it, and everyone else was doing it, so I couldn't really refuse; but now I was having second thoughts.

However, my friend Emma, who lived up the hill and along the road, had a new pony. I was trying hard, and unsuccessfully, not to be jealous.

Luckily Emma was a generous person and liked asking her friends over to ride.

I daydreamed all the time about a horse of my own, but I knew better than to get too seriously involved in that sort of fantasy. This was Cornwall, and most people's earnings were seasonal, including my father's. He taught sailing to summer visitors, and what he made in the summer had to last us the rest of the year. We never had money to spare.

"Boats are best," he tried to persuade me. "You put them away in October and forget about them until March."

"But if I had a pony, I wouldn't want to forget about it at all."

"Maybe not, but I'd soon want to forget about paying for it. Be realistic, for heaven's sake: the vet, the blacksmith, insurance, tack, feed; the list's endless. And who'd do all the work when you're at school — when you leave home in the dark, and the same at night? And where would you keep it?"

"All right; don't go on, Dad. But Emma manages it."

"It's different for her. Her parents seem to have money to splash about, and they've got a field. I hope she's prepared to work, though, because I can't see Lucinda or Brian being too interested in mucking out." He laughed. Lucinda and Brian were Emma's parents. Lucinda was large and noisy and temperamental; Brian was thin and weedy, with a cunning way of disappearing when he was needed. Dad didn't think much of either of them.

So as usual it was no use thinking about a pony; I knew it would have been different if I'd wanted a boat — any sort of boat. He'd have jumped at it then. Jonathan had his own boat now, a very small sailing dinghy. At last he'd found something to do, and nowadays when anyone asked "where's Jon?", the answer wasn't "on his bed reading a comic" or "listening to his tapes", but "out on the river" or "messing about with his boat". Mostly he disappeared quietly on his own and pottered up and down the mile-long stretch of river visible from the house, or skudded back and forth in the dumpy little dinghy, bright red sails filling, and the flat bow raising a foaming wave as it raced towards the house in the grip of a squall.

Jon was happy at last; I was glad for him, glad that he had found his own thing in life. But — I still longed for my own pony.

"When you've passed all your exams and got a really good job, then you can afford a horse of your own," Dad repeated often and boringly.

"But I'll be old then; it's *now* that's important, not when I'm old."

But Dad only laughed, and Mum looked sympathetic and changed the subject.

I remembered the evening that Emma 'phoned:

"Becky! Guess what?" she yelled down the phone,

and I had to hold it away from my ear. She was still yelling, and I had to shout back "What?" very loudly to get her to stop.

"I'm allowed a pony, I said," she continued more calmly. "I'm getting it when we find one that's the right size. Price doesn't matter too much, Dad says. What d'you think of that, then?"

I couldn't spoil Emma's excitement, but jealousy rose up and threatened to choke me. I swallowed and was silent for a moment.

"Becky?" Emma's voice was understanding. "You can come and ride as soon as I get it."

I stared at my reflection in the hall window. I did look miserable. Hardly surprising, though. Some people had all the luck. For a minute I considered my appearance: short brown hair that never went the way I wanted it to, freckled face, blue/grey eyes. Not pretty, just pretty ordinary. Perhaps I could do something better with my hair: colour it, perhaps, or grow it long, or even have it cut very short and spiked all over my head. Maybe a change would do me good. Perhaps I could have my ears pierced as well. No, Mum would never agree. Another thing that would have to wait until I was old. I sighed, and then jumped as Emma called down the phone again:

"Becky? Are you there or not?"

"Oh, sorry, I was just thinking about something else; whether to have my ears pierced, actually." I hoped this sounded casual, and that Emma wouldn't realise how much I envied her. "Well, thanks for letting me know. You *are* lucky. Let me know what happens, won't you?"

"Sure; see you soon, then." And she rang off.

That conversation seemed like ages ago; Emma had had her pony for two weeks by the time Easter arrived. It was a 12.2 hands Exmoor mare, "brown" in colour, as Emma's Dad called it. Brian knew nothing about horses, but couldn't refuse his daughter anything. Emma could wangle anything she wanted out of him.

They had called the pony Lorna, after Lorna Doone. She had the softest dark eyes imaginable, and a light-coloured velvety muzzle. She looked strong and hardy, and seemed to be an ideal first pony, very gentle and quiet, easy to catch and totally predictable. I loved her from the first as much as Emma did; more, probably, but she wasn't anything like my fantasy horse, my dream horse, my handsome glossy black stallion with shining tossing mane and tail. He would gallop boldly over the sands at low water, proudly rearing to show his fine muscles, and plunge unheeding through the shallow pools and streams, leaving showers of glittering spray behind him. I could picture it all in my head, and feel the warmth of the sun and the cool spray falling around me as I clung to his bare back, my legs wrapped around him.

But it was only fantasising.

I dressed slowly, in old jeans and a green sweater, savouring the unhurried feeling of a morning off. Homely sounds and smells reached me from the other end of the long house—the smell of warm toast and strong coffee, the sound of Mum laying the table for breakfast, the weather forecast on the radio. I felt relaxed; the days were endless, the pressures off. Spring was here—it was a new beginning, a chance to forget the dark time at Christmas. I still shuddered at the memory of the clinging muddy quicksands as I had struggled to cross the river. Cornwall was a dangerous place if you were too casual and didn't treat the sea and the river and the tides with respect. If the bait-digger hadn't appeared, I would never have made it.

But I didn't want to remember. I made a resolution. It was a bit late for a New Year's one, but an Easter one would have to do: forget Christmas, banish all thoughts of almost sinking into the quicksands—it was all over. It would be hard, but I had to do it.

The toast smelled good, different somehow. Perhaps Mum had actually bought some white bread. Her home-made brown was interesting, for want of a better word, but could be on the heavy side.

"Building a wall today, Mum?" Jonathan had been known to enquire when she turned the brick-shaped loaves out of their tins.

The phone rang, and I hurried to answer it, hoping it was Emma. It was, asking me to come over to ride Lorna. I rummaged about in my cupboard for my jodhpurs, which Mum had found at Oxfam, and my jodhpur boots. I'd had them as a wonderful present from a friend of Mum's who had come to stay. I could still feel the thrill as I opened the box and lifted them out of the white tissue paper, smooth and brown, shining like a new conker, and smelling of rich new leather.

"Can I come, Becky?" Joanna asked pleadingly. "Please, please." Red-cheeked and chubby, with two short pigtails sticking out, she could be very appealing when she was being good. "I won't be a nuisance, I promise."

I couldn't refuse. "All right, but you're *not* to be a nuisance, or Emma's Mum won't let us come again."

I went to make a picnic lunch in the kitchen, and cut some sandwiches while Joanna chattered excitedly to Mum and Dad about riding.

"They won't let you ride—you're much too young," I heard Jonathan say as he arrived for breakfast. "You'll just get in the way, and probably get kicked as well, and covered in horse manure."

"I won't!" wailed Joanna.

"And all you'll be able to do is muck out the stable, while Emma and Becky are off riding," he went on.

"It's not true! Is it, Mum?"

"Of course not," Mum replied crossly. "Don't be so spiteful, Jon, just because you're jealous."

Jonathan laughed. "Jealous? Me? Of them and some old pony? That's a joke!"

He turned to look out of the window at the river. "Boring, boring—I shan't be able to sail for hours. The tide's going out fast. I'm going back to bed. Mind you don't fall off that old nag, Becky."

And he vanished out of sight and earshot with a piece of toast in his hand.

Why did he have to be so irritating? Lorna wasn't exactly an "old nag", but it was no use pretending she was the perfect pony. Wait till I get my black stallion, I thought—then he won't be able to sneer. One day he'll find out what he's missing.

TWO
We discover the old barn

Joanna and I set off with our picnic in a haversack, up the stone steps beside the house into the orchard above, and then steeply climbing up the old footpath through the bluebell wood into the fields beyond. Joanna was persuaded to leave Brock behind. She bent down to hug him as we left, and I couldn't help feeling guilty at the sight of his black nose pressed against the window, and his dark eyes watching us out of sight.

It was a stiff climb to the top of the hill, especially for Joanna's short plump legs, and we had to stop for a breather at the edge of the orchard, looking down at the hundreds of daffodils growing amongst the grass under the fruit trees. Once this had been a smallholding, sheltered by woods on three sides, and open to the river on the fourth, and early daffodils had been sent off upcountry to market. Now they grew nearly wild, dozens of different and rare varieties making a brilliant carpet of gold and white in the midst of the leafless woodland.

After a minute Joanna and I continued our climb up the winding path between tall thin oaks and dark holly trees. Bluebells would soon be in flower, and the whole hillside a sheet of misty blue, undisturbed by winds, sheltered by the oaks which jostled each other to reach the sky, and dappled by shafts of sunlight which gilded the blue haze. This was the old church path, sometimes called the coffin path, which climbed the direct route up the hill from our house. An old thatched cottage had stood on the quay once, but nothing remained of it except two old rough stone walls which formed part of our sitting room.

The coffin path crossed one field before emerging onto the road to the church. I imagined the relief of the black-coated bearers on reaching level ground, after struggling with a heavy coffin, tilting and swaying as they heaved it up the slippery narrow path.

After climbing over the old stone stile and blinking at the sudden full daylight of the field, we galloped across the short green grass, shaking our imaginary manes and tails, letting the wind cool our flushed cheeks and tug at the flapping edges of our jackets. Joanna's pigtails tossed from side to side as she galloped, until she flopped down exhausted on the grass. I joined her and we lay on our backs watching the clouds crossing the skies above us, and the wheeling gulls circling so high that they were only specks. Far away, from the direction of the harbour, a hooter sounded mournfully, as a ship left the shelter of the land for the open sea. For a moment I wished I was on her deck, gazing towards the ocean and adventure and far-away places. Then I laughed and jumped up: "I'm glad I don't have to go sailing! Come on, Emma'll wonder where we are."

Emma's house was still more than a mile away once we reached the lane at the other side of the field. The shed where the bait-digger had lived was on our right hand side, deserted and derelict again now that he had gone. A few old buckets and tins of paint still stood in the enclosure, with long grass growing untidily over them and round the steps to the door.

I pulled Joanna's arm impatiently. "Come on, do walk a bit faster. By the time we get there it'll be time to come home."

"I'm going as fast as I can," Joanna replied crossly.

Another twenty minutes' walking brought us to Emma's house. She was watching for us at the gate, and we went into the field at the back to catch Lorna, each with a carrot which we held out to the muddy pony. Joanna ate hers while Emma wasn't looking. We spent a long time grooming Lorna, who loved to roll and cover herself with dirt, and Joanna found Emma's black kitten to play with in the straw. I combed out Lorna's mane and tail, and oiled her hooves, so she looked really smart. Then Emma and I tacked her up and led her into the yard.

"Where shall we go?" Emma asked. "What about that muddy lane? It shouldn't be too bad today, and we'll be out of the wind."

"Do we have to walk all that way?" complained Joanna. "I thought we were staying here. I don't want to walk any more."

"Don't be such a misery," I told her. "You can stay here if you like, and play with the kitten."

Then I noticed Sam coming across the yard. Sam was Emma's younger brother and Joanna's special friend.

"Look, here's Sam — you'll be OK now, and we shan't be long."

We walked Lorna out into the road, with Emma riding first. I walked alongside, and we chatted about this and that, and about younger sisters and brothers. Sam was just six, and there was a baby as well, Adam, who was still very small.

We passed the church and then looped back uphill into a narrow track, which followed the edge of the hillside, between high flower-strewn hedges, sweetly-scented, sunny and warm, now that we were sheltered from the wind. Lorna plodded on contentedly, sploshing through the muddy patches, and now and then snatching at a mouthful of tempting fresh grass from one hedge or the other. We changed places after a while, Emma giving me a leg-up on to Lorna's broad and comfortable back. It was rather like riding in a soft armchair, I thought, as I swayed rhythmically from side to side, and interesting to see over the hedge-tops into the surrounding fields, and right out to the coast in one direction. I savoured the moment, and wished disloyally that I was on my own, and preferably on my own pony.

"Sorry?" Emma was saying something.

"I wish you had a pony so that we could both ride at the same time, don't you? We could go much further, take our lunch and go for day rides. Can't you persuade your Dad?"

"No chance," I replied gloomily. "We'll never be able to afford it. Even I can see that. I'll just have to wait until I've got a proper job. Then I'll make up for all the time I've lost, and have lots of ponies and ride every day. But it won't be for years and years, will it?"

"Something may crop up. Don't give up hope. And you can come and ride Lorna with me whenever you want to, you know."

I looked down at Emma gratefully; she really was very generous. I didn't think I'd be like that if

Lorna was my pony.

"What about a little trot," Emma was asking. "Do you think you can manage?"

"Yes, of course I can," and squeezing my legs into Lorna's round sides, I urged her into a somewhat reluctant trot, which soon slowed into her favourite ambling walk again.

"You should be firmer with her," called Emma, coming up behind. "Make her do what you want her to."

"She won't. You'd better have a go," I said, pulling up in a gateway and dismounting so that Emma could take over.

Emma got Lorna trotting briskly and then urged her into a canter. They disappeared from view round the next corner. I heard the hooves pounding on the soft ground, and imagined myself galloping away into the distance on Black Magic, clearing hedges and ditches until we reached the wide open spaces of the moor, or a long white stretch of sand, lace-edged by foaming waves. Daydreaming, I wandered on, picking a few primroses and kicking stones into puddles, so that it was quite a surprise to find Emma and Lorna waiting for me at the next gateway.

"That was fun. Didn't she go well?" Emma was flushed and looking pleased. "You can ride home, Becky."

Up on Lorna's broad back again, I looked round

with interest at the views that I hadn't been able to
see whilst strolling between the high hedges. Fields
and woods stretched away on my right. Dark cloud
shadows raced across the green landscape, but in
the sheltered lane it was warm and peaceful. Half
hidden by a grove of dead elms, I spotted an old
stone building, not far ahead, over a rough grassy
field.

"What's that building?" I asked idly.

"Where? I can't see a building at all," replied
Emma, trying to peer on her toes over the hedge.

"It looks like an old barn from here. It's in a
pretty lonely spot. I wonder who it belongs to."

"I still can't see it," said Emma. "Perhaps we'll
get a better view from the next gateway, wherever
that is. I'll go ahead of you and have a look." She
walked on, Lorna following slowly, and I looked
over the hedge-top as we got nearer to the old
building. There were no windows on the side facing
the lane, or access of any kind that I could see.
There was an old wavy slate roof, with timbers
showing through in one spot, and slipped slates in
several places. Ivy covered most of one end, and a
tangle of bramble bushes grew right up to the
walls. It looked a fascinating place.

We caught up with Emma almost immediately;
she was leaning over a broken gate which seemed
to lead nowhere: just into a corner of the overgrown
field, with a spinney beyond, and the group of tall

dead trees, spiky and dark against the bright sky.

"I can't see anything," Emma said. She didn't sound very interested.

"Climb up on the gate, then you'll be nearly as high as I am," I told her.

"It's awfully ramshackle. I don't want to get caught on these broken pieces."

"Oh come on" I said impatiently. "Get up on Lorna again, and I'll climb the gate." I was getting quite good at jumping off the pony. Emma mounted again and I ran over to the gate, scrambling up the cracked cross-pieces until I could see across the field and through the spinney.

"It's an old barn, or perhaps a house. What can you see?"

"Just a roof and an old stone wall. It looks ruined to me. Come on, let's get going now, I'm getting really hungry." Emma clapped Lorna's sides with her heels and began to trot up the lane. I took one last look at the desolate place and swung down from the old gate, making it shake and wobble as I jumped off.

Emma called over her shoulder: "There's a farm up here. Perhaps they own that old barn. Probably it's not used any more. I shouldn't want to go there, though. It's awfully lonely, and I don't suppose the farmer would be too pleased if he found us trespassing."

She pulled Lorna up for me to re-mount, and

we ambled slowly up the rise at the end of the lane, rejoining the road next to a very muddy farmyard, where two large collies dashed out to bark at us, fortunately on the other side of the yard gate, scattering a selection of hens, geese and white ducks in their headlong rush.

We were both secretly relieved, I think, to emerge on to the road which led eventually to Emma's house. I felt we were back in civilisation again. Even the farmyard had looked at least a hundred years old. There were no signs of human life, and there was a strange stillness about it, despite the noisy dogs, as if it had been abandoned.

The safety of the road made me feel braver. "I'd love to explore that old barn, wouldn't you?" I asked Emma. "It looked really interesting. There might be a ghost in a place like that."

Emma looked at me shrewdly. "You don't really want to go there, do you? You can go on your own, if you do. I'm not coming, and that's final. Let me know what you find."

"I will, when I go."

"You mean if — not when." Emma sounded disbelieving and surprisingly sarcastic, for her.

I opened my mouth to retort with something hurtful in reply, but without any warning a car sped down the road towards us — braking at the sight of the pony and rider, and gently skidded to a halt a few yards ahead, tyres squealing. Lorna jumped sideways into the grass verge and reared in alarm. I clung on grimly. Lorna decided to show that she had some spirit and took off up the verge, cantering fast and tossing her head. I felt as if I was flying — this was my first canter, and once I had gathered up the reins I began to enjoy myself and pushed Lorna on until the grass gave out and there was nowhere to go except the tarmac road. By that time I had lost one stirrup, but Lorna's burst of speed was over and I was able to turn her round and walk back to meet Emma who was running up the road towards me.

"Are you OK?" Emma asked with concern. "That car was going much too fast. You did well to stay on."

"It was wonderful to go so fast! I loved it. I can't wait to canter again. Can we ride in your field next time, and maybe do some jumping as well?" I was full of enthusiasm and excitement, but Emma looked a bit doubtful. "I suppose so; but we mustn't get Lorna too hot and sweaty. It's not good for her, and she's quite old now, you know."

I sighed inwardly, still dreaming of Black Magic and imaginary gallops over the moors.

Back at Emma's house, we turned Lorna out into her field and ate our lunch sitting on bales of straw in the yard. Joanna had been playing with Sam and her hair was full of straw.

"Can I have a ride now?" she enquired while we were eating.

"No," I said, "it's too late, we're going home in a minute."

"I wanted to ride! You are mean! You promised!"

"No I didn't. It was you that wanted to come. I didn't promise anything."

"Well, I shan't come again if I can't ride," and she disappeared out of the yard and began to walk home alone.

"I'd better go," I said to Emma. "She can't walk home by herself. Thanks awfully for the ride."

"That's OK. Come up tomorrow if you're not doing anything."

"Thanks, I will. See you then." And I ran off after Joanna, who was trotting along the road, a small determined figure. I caught her up and tugged at one of her pigtails. She looked like a small scarecrow from the back, with straw sticking out of her head.

"Race you home, then?"

THREE
Disaster strikes

By the time we got home, the wind was blowing fiercely from the west, and the river was a confused jumble of breaking waves. Our moored grey dinghy pushed into them bow first, straining at its painter, corkscrewing as each passing wave lifted it over the crests. As the wind whipped round the Point opposite, great sheets of flying spray swept off the surface of the water and flew upstream and into the distance. A large cormorant surfaced, wrestling with a flat fish in its beak, tossing on the rough water, until with a final gulp, the fish vanished into the cormorant's throat.

Outside the kitchen window, a line of washing danced in the winds which swept round from either end of the house, the arms of my school shirts waving as if I was still inside them, and several pairs of jeans doing a wild dance.

"Had a good time?" Mum had heard us coming and met us at the door.

"Brilliant!" I replied. "I had a wonderful canter and managed to stay on when Lorna reared. She got frightened by a car going too fast."

Mum immediately looked worried. "Do be careful. We don't want any accidents, and you haven't been riding for very long yet. Can't you ride in the fields instead of on the road?"

"We're going to tomorrow, probably. But it's good for Lorna to get used to the roads — she might go a bit wild if she was allowed to gallop round the fields all the time."

"I didn't ride at all," Joanna complained. "It wasn't fair. I'm not going again."

"Never mind," Mum said to her in a placating way. "You stay at home with me, and we'll find something nice to do."

Brock rushed into the kitchen, twisting and jumping up in excitement. Joanna cheered up immediately. "I'll stay and play with you, Brock. You're much nicer than that old pony — but I did like the kitten."

"I had to wash all Jonathan's clothes," Mum was explaining. "He would go sailing, despite half a gale, and of course he capsized on his way back. He got home soaking wet and with the boat full of water, and he was only out for about twenty minutes. Is it worth it, I wonder?"

I shuddered: "No thanks! Not for me, anyway, but he must get some peculiar pleasure out of it, I suppose."

"It's ace today, Becky," Jonathan called from the sitting room. "Come with me later and I'll give you the thrill of your life!"

"You're not going out again today," Mum called sharply. "You'll get pneumonia and there's no-one to rescue you if you get into trouble until Dad gets home."

"Oh Mum — I won't get into trouble!"

"You don't know that, and the answer's no, anyway. Wait until tomorrow. You know Dad wants to launch the big boat if she floats early in the morning. He'll need you to help him, and you can sail with him later." Mum's voice was bright and hopeful, but there was silence from the sitting room. Out of her sight Jonathan yawned widely, and muttered "boring, boring" to himself.

In the kitchen, Mum looked at me. "He won't want to help," she said. "You know what he's like. Will you go instead? Someone'll have to."

I could feel my expression change: "But I was going riding with Emma. She's expecting me. I told you, we're riding in the field." I could see tomorrow's ride disappearing. I knew it was important for Dad to get the boat launched on the highest tide, but Jon was so awkward that he was quite capable of refusing to help. Then he appeared in the doorway, laughing. "It's all right," he said, "I'll go."

"Oh, that's great; then I can go riding again."

"Well, you don't know anything about boats. I'll make a much better job of it than you would."

I heaved a sigh of relief. I would have hated the idea of getting up at 5 a.m. on the second morning of the holidays. No doubt Jon and Dad would have launched the boat by the time I woke, and be away downriver.

But next morning Jonathan's alarm woke me promptly at 5 o'clock. It seemed to go on and on, rattling in my head until even the air seemed to be vibrating with its persistent racket. I wondered if I ought to get up to switch it off, but as the noise eventually tailed away I heard a thump as Jonathan heaved himself out of bed. I buried myself in the pillow and was just drifting off to sleep again when the bathroom door banged, rousing me again. The hall light was on, water was running. Brock jumped down off Joanna's bed and stretched out on the floor, yawning, and then scratched at the partly open door.

It was no use, I thought, I'd have to get up.

"Brock, why can't you learn how to open the door!" His tail wagged in reply. His expression was grateful, as I opened the door wide for him, his claws clicking on the boards as he trotted through.

Outside, Dad and Jonathan were already climbing

into the grey dinghy. It was hardly light. I opened the door on to the quay and to the soft dawn sounds and smells. Owls were hooting gently in the woods, and the first rooks joining in. The tide was very high already and still rising, the water flat and misty, undisturbed and unruffled. A pigeon began to call softly, and as the sky slowly lightened the garden birds joined in, until robins, chaffinches and blackbirds were all singing together. I listened spellbound, forgetting the business of launching the yacht, until a shout from Jonathan alerted me to a flying rope which landed at my feet. "Pull it in! We're away!"

I hadn't even noticed them sculling in the grey dinghy out to the floating yacht. Now her bow was turned towards the deep channel and the diesel engine was thumping dully. I watched the yacht's progress as she slipped away from her winter berth, heading eagerly downstream and towards the freedom of the harbour. Jonathan and Dad waved briefly, moving about on deck, busy with ropes and fenders.

Brock stared wistfully after them — he was a keen ship's dog. "Your turn'll come, Brock." I patted him consolingly. "You can go next time." He turned up his head sideways to look at me, his dark eyes eager. "Come on, back to bed."

I collected a cup of tea from the pot in the kitchen, but knew I wouldn't sleep again. Joanna was still sleeping soundly. Brock settled himself against her — they looked like two small animals curled together. I quietly drew the curtains back and sat in the early morning light reading a pony book, now and again looking out at the deep water outside the window and marvelling that in six hours or less I would be able to cross to the boat-house on the opposite bank on foot if I wanted to. But I didn't, not yet. I was going right away from the river to ride with Emma.

I left the house on my own after breakfast, and arrived at Emma's just as she was getting out of bed.

"She won't be long," called Lucinda from the kitchen window. "You go and catch Lorna and Emma'll be out as soon as she's eaten something. She had a bit of a lie-in this morning, so nothing's been done."

"Don't blame her," I called, heading for the paddock. Lorna lifted her head at my call, and came eagerly over for her carrot. She stood quietly munching while I put the head collar on, and then followed agreeably as I led her into the stable to put on her tack. It was warm and friendly in there, and I felt pleased but guilty to be alone with Lorna. I learned against the soft neck and wished the placid pony was my own and not Emma's.

The quiet moment was shattered by the arrival of Sam: "Where's Joanna?" he demanded, banging into the stable and making Lorna jump sideways, treading on my toes and almost sending me flying against the wall.

"Don't make such a noise, Sam, for goodness sake, unless you want to get trampled — like I've just been," I added, hopping about on one foot and anxiously looking down at my jodhpur boot. I was much more worried about it than about my foot, but there was only a slight mark showing on the shiny leather.

"Well, where is she?" Sam persisted. "Isn't she here? She said she was coming today." Without waiting for me to reply, he stamped out into the yard again, making as much noise as before. Lorna watched him go with soft reproachful eyes. I sighed ... brothers!

Lorna was dry, and the mud came off her easily, in clouds, pricking my eyes and falling into my hair and my sweater. She stood still while I groomed her until her coat shone, combed out her mane and tail, and picked out her hooves. I tacked her up and led her out, and was just about to mount when Emma arrived, looking immaculate in clean black jodhpurs, white sweat shirt, and polished black jodhpur boots. Her skull cap was covered with a gorgeous lavender silk. It looked new. She looked amazing.

My Oxfam jodhpurs were a faded beige colour and getting tight. I hadn't got a silk for my skull cap, which was a spare one of Emma's. At least my new boots still glowed, but for a minute I felt like the paid hand, holding the pony ready for Emma to mount.

But generous as ever, Emma said, "I'll hold her for you Becky. You ride first as you've done all the work. Where shall we go today?"

I mounted quickly, feeling ashamed of my jealousy. I was a scrap too big for Lorna if I was honest. My legs were slightly too long, but at least I wasn't overweight.

"What about the bottom lane and along by the stream? We're not likely to meet any cars there."

"Good idea."

We walked out into the road and past the church as before, but then ignored the turn into the track that we had taken the day before, continuing to the foot of the hill where an ancient bridge crossed a fast-flowing stream. There were a few cottages on either side of the bridge, but no-one about, and we turned left along a tiny winding lane, canopied with hazel trees and drooping catkins, and noisy with the rushing water alongside. I dismounted here for Emma to take over, and Lorna ambled along in the dappled sunlight, while we chatted companionably. The lane became narrower and more shady, damp at each side where water trickled down towards the sinuous dark stream which ran beside.

"I shouldn't want to come here alone," I remarked. "It's so quiet, but at the same time you can't hear anything round you except the noise of the water. Even Lorna's hooves seem muffled and echoing, somehow."

"I've never been this far along here before," Emma said. "I don't know where it comes out, do you?"

"No, not really, but we'll go on and see, shall we?"

"All right; if you really want to."

We wandered along slowly, looking out for a gateway or track leading off that we could take, rather than going home the same way. Interlocking branches criss-crossed over our heads, blocking out the sky, and on either side now the hedges were thick and impenetrable, a tangled mass of bramble, holly and hazel, which seemed to close in on us.

"I'm not too keen on this." Emma spoke nervously in a low voice. "Shall we turn round and go back?"

"Lorna's quite happy. She'd sense if there was anything wrong, and if she was frightened we'd soon know about it—she just wouldn't go on, would she? Let's carry on a bit further. It's exciting to see where it leads."

Reluctantly, Emma urged Lorna forwards, and away from a clump of damp lush grass that had caught the pony's eye.

The little narrow lane snaked round a tight corner ahead of us, and as if by magic, a gap appeared in the undergrowth on our left, and an old pointing sign proclaimed "Bridleway" in faded lettering, directing us across a planked footbridge into a tangle of small trees. It looked soft and muddy underfoot, but not far off we could see brightness as the trees thinned.

"Just our luck!" I exclaimed. "Just exactly what we wanted!"

"I wonder where it goes, though," Emma queried, dismounting hurriedly. "We don't want to get lost."

"It doesn't really matter where it goes. We shall get home eventually, and look—Lorna wants to go this way." The pony had stepped off the stony surface of the lane and was already picking her way delicately over the planks of the footbridge, pulling Emma with her. I followed, and Lorna led us through the spindly trees of an old copse until we emerged into the daylight at the end of a long narrow meadow, bordered on one side by the stream, which had twisted back on itself somehow. Behind the stream the land rose steeply, as it did on the other side of the meadow, where the ground was disturbed and pitted with what looked like huge holes and mounds of earth clinging to the slope.

"Look, it must be an enormous badger sett," I said, pointing it out to Emma. "What a hideaway for them — this lovely meadow to play in, and the stream running alongside. I wonder if there are any footprints at the edge of the water." I wandered along the level turfy bank, now and then stepping down on to small gravelly beaches.

"It's like a huge waterway in miniature," I called to Emma, who was tying Lorna to a tree. "I wish we had some boats to sail."

"How old are you?" Emma looked at me pityingly. "It looks like a perfectly normal stream to me. I suppose you'd like to see it lined with garden gnomes with their fishing rods."

"You haven't a scrap of imagination," I retorted crossly, walking further along the bank. Then — "look!" I shouted, "Masses of paw marks! There must be badgers. This is where they cross. Can you see the scrape marks on the other side? And there's a big tree trunk where they scratch. There could be dozens here."

"Wait till I tell my Dad," said Emma in excitement.

"No, no, you mustn't tell anyone they're here!"

"Why ever not?"

"Because the more people that know, the more likely it is that someone will come and shoot them or gas them, or poison them, or bait them with dogs. We couldn't ever bring Brock here either, in case he went down one of the holes and started to fight with one of them. Then we'd have to dig him out; sometimes terriers stay down for hours. Sometimes they get trapped or injured or killed and never come out."

Emma's eyes were wide with amazement: "Are the badgers down there now?" she said, looking over towards the sett. "Can they hear us talking?"

"I expect so. They'll be very wary when they come out tonight. They'll still be able to smell us even when we've gone."

"Can't I even tell Mum?"

"No — you mustn't tell anyone. Promise?"

"If you say so," Emma answered doubtfully. "I can keep a secret. Can you, though?"

"Of course." I was offended. "Better than anyone I know."

"How do you know that? That's not logical. If people can keep secrets no-one else knows they've got them, do they?"

"Oh, I don't know," I said, jumping up abruptly from where I'd been sitting watching the water. "I wish we had something to drink; it's so hot and airless here. Do you think we could drink from the stream?"

"No, of course not." Emma was horrified. "You don't know what's been in it further upstream. Lorna could have a drink though. Shall we let her graze for a little while? She can't go anywhere if we watch her."

"OK — I'll take her saddle off to give her a rest."
I placed the saddle carefully on a tussock of short grass and knotted the reins loosely on her neck so that she could graze. She moved slowly about the shady side of the meadow, placidly feeding. When she reached the stream she stepped down on to the gravelly strip at the side of the water, and dipped her muzzle into the flowing bubbling shallows, then resumed her grazing, with droplets falling from her mouth and nose.

I watched her and thought what a contented pony she was. Even my own simple life seemed a tangle of difficulties compared with Lorna's basic needs of grass and water.

Emma and I sat chatting on the grass.

"Tonight's the start of the sponsored fast, don't forget," I said without enthusiasm. "I'm not much looking forward to it. I'm going to eat a huge meal tonight. I don't know how I'm going to manage not to eat from seven this evening until the same time tomorrow — twenty four hours without food! I wonder if the starving children in Ethiopia realise what we're doing for them?"

"I don't suppose they do for a moment," Emma replied. "How much money have you raised so far? I've got twelve pounds fifty already, and lots of people that I haven't asked yet."

"I've got about five pounds, and I don't think

there's anyone else to ask."

"What about your neighbours — the Fieldings?"

"Yes, I suppose I could go to them, and the other people further down the river, but I don't much like asking them."

"Why not?" Emma was surprised.

"Well, I don't mind asking my family, and my friends at school, although that's a bit pointless because they ask me, and then we all end up sponsoring each other, and usually they don't pay up. Mum says you can't ask the neighbours too often or they don't like it."

"I should think they'd be pleased to help."

"I'm not looking forward to it, anyway. Do you think we'll lose much weight in a day without eating?"

"Maybe a couple of pounds," Emma replied. "Except we'll be so starving by tomorrow evening that we'll eat loads and put it all back on again."

"Come on, then," I said, jumping up. "Let's get going and see where this valley leads to, shall we?"

Lorna had strayed over to the other side of the meadow, near the badger sett. I ran over to her, caught the reins and unknotted them. Drawing the pony near to the grassy rise which led up to the sett, I got a firm foothold and launched myself on to Lorna's broad bare back.

"I feel like an Indian squaw," I called across to Emma, who was waiting with the saddle. I bounced up and down and sideways as Lorna broke into a slow trot.

"Very elegant," Emma said, laughing as we came up to her and I slid off.

"I think I'd have fallen off if she hadn't stopped," I said. "She's awfully bouncy and I was sliding from side to side. You can't get a grip with your legs, can you?"

"Oh, I don't know," Emma replied casually. "You can when you get used to riding bareback. I sometimes do when I bring her in from the field."

"Go on then," I suggested. "Have a go now. It's lovely here, so deserted, and it feels just like the Wild West. My brother likes Westerns, and they always ride bareback in those films. I can just imagine hundreds of Indians on their ponies galloping down this valley towards us, waving their bows and arrows and shouting war cries."

"You just want to be carried off by a handsome Indian brave." Emma was laughing at me.

"No I don't," I denied hotly. "I was just picturing a scene from a film, that's all. Go on, you have a go bareback now."

I gave Emma a leg-up and slapped Lorna on the hindquarters. Lorna obligingly ambled off, Emma sitting comfortably on her broad back while she walked down the meadow.

"Faster than that!" I called after them, running to catch them up. "Make her trot!" I let out what I thought was an Indian war cry, and Lorna jumped, startled by the noise, and settled into a reluctant trot. Emma bounced about, her legs flapping, trying to keep a proper seat.

"That's better," I called. "Go on up the meadow and then bring her back faster!"

Emma slowed the pony and then turned her back towards me. With the long expanse of grass before her, and the prospect of going home, Lorna didn't need any urging, and was soon breaking into an enthusiastic canter. Emma clung on to the reins and then to Lorna's mane, and I watched in admiration as they covered the full length of the meadow, only slowing at the far end by the gap in the bushes where we had come in from the lane.

"Well done! Well done!" I shouted, and Emma grinned with pleasure. "I'll do it again!" she called, and clapped her legs into Lorna's sides.

But Lorna thought they were heading for home, and wasn't keen to repeat her Indian pony performance for the fun of it. She tossed her head and tugged the reins out of Emma's hands, trotted a few paces back into the meadow, and then wheeled round and plunged forward, kicking up her heels and unseating Emma, who lost her grip on Lorna's mane and flew off sideways and downwards, landing awkwardly on one leg, before crumpling to the ground with a sharp cry of pain.

Lorna had disappeared through the gap in the

hedge by the time I reached the end of the meadow. I ran up to Emma, who was still lying on the ground, her face white and twisted with pain.

"What have you done? Where does it hurt?" I stammered, frightened.

"It's my leg; I can't move it. It's agony." Emma's face was white, and creased with pain, as she tried to stretch her leg out from the unnatural way it was lying.

"Lie back a minute," I said. "I'll see if I can straighten it for you, and then it'll feel better."

"No, it hurts too much," Emma wailed, but she leaned back on one elbow while I gently lifted her leg and straightened it. When it was done, Emma gave a sort of sobbing gasp, and flopped backwards on to the grass.

"Is it broken, do you think? It hurts like mad. Where's Lorna? I'll never get home like this." Her eyes were huge and dark and frightened in her white face, and she had begun to shake with shock.

"Here, have my sweater," I said, and pulled it off over my head, then covering Emma as best as I could. I stared down at the damaged leg, afraid to touch it.

"It feels awfully tight and hot inside my boot," Emma said miserably. "I think I ought to take it off if I can."

"Let's have a go, then. And afterwards I'll go

and look for Lorna. Be brave!" Trying to look
confident but feeling worried, I started to slide
Emma's jodhpur boot over her ankle. It wouldn't
have been so bad if it had laced up, but the elastic
sides didn't stretch easily, and I knew that it must
be hurting badly. I wriggled and pulled as carefully
as I could, not looking at Emma, and trying to
ignore her gasps of pain. I knew the boot would
have to come off, as the leg was looking very
puffy round the ankle already, and was sure to get
worse.

At last the boot came off with a bit of a jolt, and
Emma flopped flat on the grass, her face screwed
up and her eyes shut, looking awful. I wondered
desperately what to do next. I'd have to leave
Emma if I went to search for Lorna; if I didn't get
the pony back I'd never be able to get Emma
home.

I brought the saddle over to where Emma lay
and pillowed her head on it as carefully as I could.
It didn't look very comfortable, but it was better
than lying flat on the ground. I tucked my sweater
round her top half. Luckily she was lying in the
sun and the grass was dry. Despite the warmth I
shivered with the fright of it all in my thin T-shirt.

"Lie still," I told Emma. "I'll be back as soon as
I can, with Lorna I hope. She can't have gone far,
and then we can get you home."

"I certainly won't be going anywhere." Emma made an effort to joke, and watched me out of sight, looking small and scared and lonely stretched out in the deserted valley.

FOUR
The stranger in the lane

I pushed through the spiky branches until I reached
the footbridge. The pony's hoof marks were clearly
visible in the damp earth, but once on the lane
they vanished. I searched around in one direction
and then the other until I picked up Lorna's trail
leading out of a damp patch. There were human
bootmarks as well, quite new ones, still wet. I ran
on. Lorna had turned along the lane in the direction
we had come from in the first place, probably
making her way home, sensibly. But I wanted her
to stop — I needed her to transport Emma home. I
willed her to stop. I hoped desperately that I
wouldn't have to find other help. It would delay
things so much if I had to start knocking on those
silent cottage doors and making long explanations,
even if I could find anybody at home.

I was racing with the flow of the rushing stream
as it bubbled along beside me, the noise of the
water and the thumping of my heart muffling any
other sounds. I rounded a curve in the lane and
halted abruptly with a gasp as I almost ran into
Lorna standing broadside across the track, blocking
my way. What scared me was the man who held
her — possessively, almost as if he owned her —
staring at me over her back. I was dizzy with
running and almost fell over my own feet. His
deep-set shadowy eyes met mine, watching me, as
he stood his ground, at ease with the pony. She
wasn't fidgeting or fretting to be off. I wondered if
he would have disappeared with her if I hadn't
come along. They could have melted into the
countryside together and never been seen again.

The stranger seemed to blend with the background in the oddest way — gnomelike, with a lined
brown face, almost like a small wiry tree — part of
the scenery. Clothes to match, brown and leathery,
creased.

I wanted to leave, quickly — it was no place to
meet a stranger. I'd been warned enough times
about that sort of situation. I thought about Emma
lying in the field, and summoned enough courage
to grasp Lorna's reins tightly and pull her back the
way I had come. She was strangely reluctant to
move, and I felt the man's watching eyes as I
tugged at her head.

"Come on, for heaven's sake!" I muttered, and my voice sounded strange and nervous, though I had spoken softly. Something stopped me completely from speaking to him — some sense of his strangeness. Perhaps he clapped Lorna on her hindquarters, or perhaps he just allowed her to go, I don't know. Maybe I imagined the low laugh, but suddenly she began to follow me, both of us running back up the lane. Not daring to look round, I prayed the man wasn't following. I slowed briefly when I came to a place at the side of the road where I could step up easily onto the bank, and barely stopping Lorna, I threw myself over her back and somehow got into a sitting position, risking a quick glance behind at the same time.

The man had vanished as if he had never existed; there was just no sign of him following. There were no hiding places along the lane, a steep sloping hillside on one hand, and the bank and stream on the other.

I sighed with relief, shaking a little, heart thudding, and clicked my tongue to Lorna, who obediently broke into a trot. I battled with the effort of staying on and was thankful when we reached the footbridge on our left. We trotted through the spinney where pricking branches caught at my face and hair, but I brushed them aside and with tremendous relief saw that Emma was still lying in the same spot, watching for us, half raised on her elbow, her dark hair glinting in the sunlight, almost as if she was sunbathing. But — the black jodhpurs were immaculate no longer and the white sweat shirt was streaked with muddy stains. Strands of hair clung clammily to her forehead. Her face was chalk white, and, as I dismounted, I could see that her eyes were clouded with pain and she looked tearful: "Thank goodness you found her; she must have been miles away, you've been ages."

"Sorry — she wasn't far off. A man had caught her. I don't know who he was, but he was holding her, only about half way along the lane."

Emma looked more upset than before. "I hope he won't come this way," she said nervously, looking over towards the gap in the trees. "I'd have been terrified if I'd thought there was anyone around when I was lying here alone."

"Don't worry about it." I hoped I sounded reassuring. "He's gone the other way. Now we've got to try and get you up onto Lorna's back. I'll just get the saddle on and then give you a heave." I said this with more confidence that I felt, and my misgivings were confirmed when I had to almost lift Emma to her feet and then push her up into the saddle. With several heaves from me, and with great difficulty, Emma was mounted on Lorna, but every movement brought tears and groans, and I had to be firm with her — cruel to be kind —

or Emma would have collapsed into a limp heap again.

Once on the pony, and with her right leg dangling, Emma held on tightly to the reins and allowed me to lead her along the peaceful valley bottom. Her face was tearstained and white, and I hoped it wouldn't be too far before we emerged onto the road once more. I hardly knew where we were, although I felt we were going in the right direction to circle back to Emma's house quicker than retracing our steps along the bottom lane, and the thought of meeting the man again put me off that route.

There had been something very weird about him. Not exactly sinister — I couldn't put it into words — but it wasn't an exaggeration to admit to myself that he had scared me. The mocking look in the deep eyes hadn't all been imagination. And he hadn't spoken. Odd . . .

"It must be awfully late," Emma was saying. "Mum will be really worried by now, especially as she didn't know where we were going. She'll be sending out a search party. She'll be furious . . . What an awful end to our ride. I don't feel at all safe; go slowly, Becky. My leg's hurting so much, every time Lorna takes a step it hurts more." She slumped in the saddle, her head drooping, just longing to be home, I could tell.

"At least it's a bit of an adventure," I said brightly,

and tactlessly. "Not knowing where we are and . . ."
my voice tailed off, and I could have bitten my
tongue off as I spoke.

Emma lifted her head and stared at me. "You
don't mean we're lost?" she wailed. "Don't you
know where we are? You brought us here — you
must know! We'll never get home, I know we
won't. I can't bear it much longer, I just want to
go home." The tears began to fall in earnest, and I
patted her leg awkwardly.

"Cheer up — you're making Lorna look upset. I
promise we'll get back soon. Look, isn't that the
church tower? We can't be far as the crow flies."

"But Lorna's not a crow — she's a lazy naughty
pony and if she hadn't thrown me off this wouldn't
have happened."

I sighed, and gave up trying to be cheerful, and
we ambled on across the field, following the line
of the stream, which had shrunk to only a trickle
now. A flock of sheep and lambs were scattered
over the field ahead of us, and the lambs ran bleating
to their mothers at the sight of the pony. I felt I
had been here before, although I knew I hadn't.
We were out in the open now, and looking to my
left where the ground rose gently to the church,
poised on the top of the ridge in the distance, I
suddenly realised that we were crossing ground
that we had been looking at the day before when
we were trying to see the deserted barn. I shaded

my eyes and scanned the slope, looking for a grove of dead elms.

The sun was in my eyes, but I soon picked out the bare elms, sheltering the low-lying building on all sides. It was no more obvious from here than it had been from the other direction. On this side, looking into the valley, there appeared to be a large doorway, dark, as if the door was open or off its hinges, and a smaller door, and maybe a small high window, although the whole building was surrounded and almost covered by under-growth, and wouldn't even be noticed at a casual glance.

Lorna stumbled suddenly, jerking the reins out of my grasp, and Emma's moan of pain brought me back to the present. I searched for encouraging words again: "Look, we must be getting nearer to home. I think we should take the next gate out of here and then turn left and head for the church tower." Emma didn't reply. She looked awful, white-faced and drooping in the saddle, holding Lorna's mane with limp fingers. I was afraid she might slip sideways at any minute, and kept glancing at her anxiously.

By some stroke of luck our ordeal was almost over. We were no sooner through the next gate and starting to climb the slope which led back towards the church, another tiny lane hedged steeply with wild flowers and tangled grasses, when a blue tractor appeared ahead, rumbling down towards us. The driver slowed and stopped when he saw the pony, and Lorna shied nervously, knocking me against the bank. Emma hung on grimly, biting her lip, as I quietened Lorna. As the driver climbed down from the cab and came towards us, I called, "Can you help us? There's been an accident and my friend's hurt her leg."

Luckily the driver recognised Emma, and was helpful enough to lift her down and carry her to the tractor, just squeezing past to deposit her in a sitting position on the small platform at the back. She held tightly to the sides, her face ashen, looking small and vulnerable. "Don't tell anyone that we were riding bareback," she whispered to me. "I'd get into awful trouble if Mum found out. You said you could keep a secret. You will, won't you?" She looked pleadingly at me, and I had a vision of her mum, large and noisy and a bit overpowering at close quarters. I knew it would be a mistake to get on the wrong side of Lucinda.

"I won't say anything to anyone," I promised, and Emma looked relieved.

"You can get Lorna home, can't you?"

"Yes, of course. See you soon! Don't go and fall off and do the other leg in, will you?"

Emma raised a wan smile as I slid past the tractor to where I had abandoned Lorna in the lane. Luckily she had stayed where I'd left her, snatching greedily at anything green in the hedge. I led her back a short distance while the driver started up the tractor and backed up the hill, disappearing with a rumble and a cloud of smoke, turning to wave reassuringly to me as he vanished out of sight.

I was alone with Lorna in the peaceful deserted lane. I wished the day was just beginning, and that the pony and I were free to go where we pleased. I spun out the ride back to Emma's house, but too soon we arrived and turned into the yard, to be greeted by a wide-eyed Sam.

"Emma's going to hospital and we're going too! Mum's on the phone now. What happened? You've been away for hours! Mum was just going out in the car to search for you, but she didn't know where you'd gone. She's not very pleased," he added ominously, and suddenly I shivered in my thin T-shirt. Everything was ruined, especially if Lucinda stopped us from riding, which she was quite likely to do.

"Sam! Sam!" Lucinda's voice shouted from the garage behind the wall, and a car door slammed at the same time as its tyres crunched across the gravel. A green estate car came into view and stopped in the yard, Emma sitting in the front passenger seat looking forlorn and as if she'd been crying. In the back was a wailing baby, strapped in and struggling in its seat — Adam.

"Sam, get in!" his mother called, leaning back to

open the door, her plumpish face red and harrassed.

"This I could do without!" she called over to
me. "I've got enough to do without having to
drop everything and rush to the hospital, with
these other two horrors in tow, not to mention the
dog." Then I noticed the bulky form of the Old
English Sheepdog, trying to lick away Adam's
tears from behind the dog guard. It was making
him yell and struggle worse than before, but no-
one took any notice.

Lucinda had to shout louder. "I suppose you can
see to the wretched pony, can you?"

"Yes, of course," I replied. "And I'm really sorry
about Emma. I hope it's not too serious. It wasn't
her fault, really it wasn't." Was it, or wasn't it? I
wondered, crossing my fingers unobtrusively in
case it was.

"Then whose fault was it?" Lucinda shouted
above the noise of the car and the baby.

"Oh, never mind," I heard her say finally, looking
at my miserable face, and relenting a little. She put
the car into gear again, noisily, and gave me a
scanty wave. Emma gave me what might have
passed for a smile under happier circumstances.
Adam was still howling, and the dog turned round
to bark at me as the car lurched across the gravel,
scattering stones.

"Good luck," I called, but they were already
turning into the road and no-one heard me. I was

left standing staring at the empty yard, Lorna's reins still in my hand.

I gave the pony a rub down and a carrot, and turned her out into the field. Watching her over the gate, grazing lazily on the short grass, unaware of the drama, I thought: well, that's that. I don't suppose I'll be asked over to ride for ages, if ever. Everything's changed just because we risked riding bareback and Emma managed to fall off. I started it — I suppose that makes it my fault that it went wrong.

Lorna was down on the grass, her front legs sinking under her and the back ones following, rolling and rolling from side to side, legs waving cheerfully in the air, on the flattened patch that she always used. She heaved herself upright again and had a good shake, as if shaking off her troubles. I wished I could do that, give myself a shake and get back to normal. Oh how I wished I could turn the clock back, back beyond the catastrophic events of the morning!

FIVE
Bad news

"Well, do just that—turn the clock back," Mum suggested later, when I had poured out the events of the morning to her understanding ears, carefully omitting the fact that we had been riding bareback, more for Emma's sake than my own, I tried to convince myself. I also thought it wiser not to mention the man who had caught Lorna in the lane.

"How do I do that?" I asked without much interest. "It sounds impossible to me."

"Just pretend it didn't happen. Make a fresh start. Do something else!"

"I can't pretend it didn't happen—Emma's hurt. Her Mum was pretty annoyed. I don't suppose she'll let me forget about it in a hurry, and I pity poor Emma."

"Lucinda's not as bad as all that—she must have been worried, don't forget. I'm sure it'll all blow over before you know it."

"But if Emma's broken her ankle we won't be able to ride again these holidays, so what am I going to do for two weeks? Nothing!"

Mum considered: "Well, you could go off in the boat with Dad and Jonathan for a few days. They'd love you to go along."

I stared at her and shook my head emphatically. "No, no, no! That's the last thing I'd want to do."

"Well, just so long as you know you can, any time."

"I don't want to, you know I don't, so it's no use suggesting it."

"Easter Day tomorrow—you can help me hide the little chocolate eggs."

My face was scornful now, but I didn't care. "Mum, remember I am nearly thirteen, not three."

I went disconsolately to the other end of the house, finding that Joanna had spread her dolls all over my bed, and the room was in a complete mess. I backed out again, and for once wished Jonathan was there to talk to. Then I noticed Brock—he had made a comfortable nest on Joanna's pillow, and was watching me hopefully.

"Come on then, let's go!" His company would be best of all at the moment: totally undemanding. We walked upstream on the shingle and pebbles that edged the estuary, keeping away from the sheet of mud which sloped away to the tidal stream beyond. I gloomily kicked a stone or two, unable to throw off the cloud which seemed to have settled on me. Horses were my only interest now. Without them I felt nearly as bad as I supposed Jon had felt before he had discovered boats. Life seemed to have no purpose. The holidays which had started so promisingly held little attraction for me any more. Emma and I had planned so many rides and picnics, and jumping practice in the field.

Brock had caught my mood and was trotting docilely by my side, now and then glancing up and into my face, trying to read my expression. He looked so comical with one ear up and the other flopped forward and his head on one side, almost as if he could speak. I knew just what his voice would sound like if he did.

"Sorry," I said to him, bending to pick up a stick. "Sorry I'm so boring." He immediately looked more cheerful and began to prance about, barking excitedly. I flung the stick ahead and he chased it along the shore, snatching it up without stopping his headlong rush, and galloping away from me with the stick held awkwardly at one end in his pointed jaws. Two fat brown and white shelduck waddled rapidly away ahead, making their funny whistling and croaking noises, one jerking its head up and down in what it thought was a menacing manner. Brock dropped the stick and rushed towards them, barking as they took flight across the river.

I caught Brock up at a picturesque grassy promontory, where a group of ancient stones ran down into the channel. One very large upright stone was set in the grass; other smaller ones descended into the stream. This place was known as the Hen and Chickens, the Hen being the largest stone, and was a popular picnic spot with local people and holidaymakers. A strong rope hanging from an oak branch made a swing, and burnt patches in the grass were left from barbecue parties. I sat down on one of the Chickens, gazing down the river to where I could see a few masts out in mid-channel, the first of the yachts to appear on their moorings this season. Rather them than me, I thought, mentally already resisting the attempts Dad was sure to make to persuade me to go sailing with him. He could be very persuasive though.

The welcoming smell of baking greeted me at the kitchen door when I got back.

"What are you making?" I asked Mum, trying to make up for my previous rudeness.

"Easter cake," was the reply, "I saved the bowl for you to scrape."

"I want to scrape it!" Joanna came running. "Let me!"

"No, it's Becky's turn—you can decorate the

top with eggs and the chicken when it's cool. Look, I've saved this little yellow chick since last year. I couldn't bear to throw him away."

I scraped the bowl like Mum wanted me to, but I knew that mooning about the place wasn't going to do any good — that was just a waste of time. But what could I do ...? I gazed out of the large picture window: a young single swan was gliding past on the last of the ebbing tide. A black cormorant's head popped up just ahead of it, and it stretched its neck and flapped its large dark wings almost in the swan's face, and then took off, leaving the swan swinging round to stare after it in surprise.

The waste of sand in the bed of the river reminded me of my dream horse, Black Magic. The very sight of him would scatter the seabirds. Clouds of gulls would rise at the sound of his thundering hooves. I could hear him galloping, just out of sight. Any second he would come into view ...

But it was only a train — a train loaded with china clay, rumbling down to the docks on the single railway line which ran alongside the far bank of the estuary. I jerked myself back to reality. Joanna and Mum were chattering in the kitchen about cakes and Easter eggs and chickens. Dad and Jonathan would be back on the rising tide. I had to go out before then, before all the talk was of boats

and sailing, sailing and boats, and I was either
almost screaming with irritation or yawning my
head off with boredom.

I could have cried when I remembered the
gymkhana. Emma had promised that I could come
with her to the next one, and enter as many classes
as she did on Lorna. They were held every three
weeks and sounded great fun. We could have ridden
there from Emma's. It was only an hour or so to
ride to our nearest small town where they were
held. The first of the season would have been the
next weekend, and it would have been a first
attempt — the first of many, I hoped — for both of
us.

Part of me wanted to hear the news about
Emma's leg. I was hoping desperately that she
wasn't too badly hurt. But the other part of me
dreaded the sound of the telephone and the bad
news that it might bring. I walked about, backwards and forwards through the house, watching
the phone each time I crossed the hall, waiting for
it to ring and break the suspense. Why wouldn't it
ring? Why? They must be back from the hospital
by now. But it didn't.

"Stop pacing about," Mum called. "Haven't you
got anything to do?"

"No, nothing at all."

"Do you want a job?"

"No." I knew I sounded churlish and rude.

Wisely perhaps she left me alone, and I was grateful. I still stood, staring out at the river and wooded hillside opposite, the first spring green appearing amongst the winter bareness. I heard whispering from the kitchen, and Joanna came out, calling "Becky ...", "stopping abruptly when she saw me standing at the window.

"What?" I asked unkindly, and in an instant the smile vanished from her cheerful chubby face, making me feel worse than before.

"I was going to ask if you'd take me out," she said in a woebegone way, "but not if you don't want to." I relented, hating myself for my bad temper and this aimless feeling that I couldn't shake off. "Where shall we go?" I asked, and was rewarded by the brightening of her face, and an equally bright smile from Mum, who put her head round the kitchen door to give me an approving look.

"Let's just go," Joanna said. "It doesn't matter where, and can I take my bike?"

My heart sank — that meant I'd have to push it up the hill. But all I said was, "OK, if you really want to. Let's go." I was making a real effort to be patient with her, although I didn't know how long I could keep it up. But I had to do something. As well as Emma, there was the prospect of the twenty-four hour fast beginning that night. I dreaded it, and bitterly regretted having agreed to take part. I hoped Mum would produce something really special and filling for supper so that I could stuff myself.

"Remember I can't eat after seven, Mum," I called to her as we left. "Can we eat at six so that I have an hour to fill myself up?"

"I was hoping you'd forgotten that, Becky. I think it's a really ridiculous idea."

"Me too, but I've got to do it now that I've been promised the money."

I wasn't going to push Joanna up the hill on her bike, so she insisted on pushing one handlebar while I took the other, which made it ten times as difficult. We stopped at each of the three gateways to have a rest and to survey the fields and river valley laid out beneath us. Half way up we met a car coming down and had to lean backwards into the hedge with the bike on top of us to let the car pass. The lane was never meant for cars in the first place — horses, perhaps . . .

It was one of our neighbours, Denis Fielding. He stopped the car and leaned over to wind down the window. "Hi girls! Enjoying your holiday, Becky?" He always made a special effort to be nice to me, because of me getting his stolen property back at Christmas. By my bed was the clock radio that he and his wife Dorothy had bought me as a present, a sort of reward. That had helped a lot at the time, because I was pretty upset afterwards.

"Yes thanks, Denis. It's great not to have to go to school." He liked to be called Denis—I suppose it made him feel younger. He was nice really, even though he was getting on a bit. And I wasn't enjoying my holiday at all, but only I understood why, so it was no use saying so.

He waved goodbye and drove on down the hill. We were almost at the top, and soon Joanna was able to ride. She went on alone and round the first corner, leaving me with my thoughts.

Mum had promised me a new pair of jodhpurs for the gymkhana, and I mean a brand-new pair. I wouldn't get them now. I wouldn't even need the old ones if I wasn't going to ride any more. Someone else might like them, third hand. But I couldn't part with my precious boots. I'd keep them for when I rode Black Magic . . .

Fantasising again! A faint tinkling noise brought me down to earth, and I turned round to see Brock at full stretch, racing towards me, tongue hanging out, ears and fur swept back. The tinkle of his name disc on the collar was a good warning of his approach, especially to cats and birds. Mum must have let him out of the house after we left, and then he had followed our scent up the hill. We had no lead with us, but at the top of the hill was a roadsign where we had hidden a length of twine for this purpose, so I caught his collar and held him, still panting, while I found the twine which did service for a lead, to keep him from chasing wandering chickens and cats, or cars.

Joanna was waiting for me at the end of the lane. Brock was so delighted to see her that he almost knocked her off the bike in his excitement. I pulled him away and we carefully crossed to the other side of what we called the main road, and headed towards Emma's house. The road was barely wide enough for two cars to pass, and most drivers flew along it far too quickly, probably because it was slightly wider than the tiny lanes leading off it, most of which were about six feet wide and had grass growing up the middle, looking as if they led nowhere. Visitors to this part of Cornwall were usually astonished at the narrow lanes, and always getting lost.

At Emma's drive, we looked about for the car, but everywhere seemed deserted. We crossed the yard and leaned on the gate watching Lorna grazing in her usual placid way. I found I had some mints in my pocket, and called her, and she ambled over in our direction. Joanna climbed up a couple of bars and held a mint out for her to take, and we made a fuss of her for a few minutes.

We were just thinking of going home, when I heard a car slowing down, and the green estate car swung into the drive. I raised my arm to wave, but quickly dropped it again as a sad sight met my eyes. Propped against some cushions in the back of the estate car — the very back where the luggage and dogs go — was Emma, her legs stretched out, and her right one encased in a huge white plaster cast, the leg of her black jodhpurs cut right off or slit down — I couldn't see which — and her bare foot protruding from the end of the plaster. Her hands were gripping the back of the seat and the door frame beside her and she looked completely immobile.

This was the worst thing I could possibly have imagined. I warned Joanna to keep quiet, and quickly tied Brock to the gate, hoping he wouldn't see the huge sheepdog, who had been squeezed into the front seat and was already scratching to get out. I didn't intend to be seen at this stage. Luckily Joanna hadn't seen Emma, being too engrossed with the pony, and thought it was some kind of game of hide and seek that I was playing, so she obligingly kept out of sight. I moved across to the wall that divided the yard from the garage and the back of the house, and carefully looked over, hiding behind a climbing rose bush. Emma's Dad, Brian, had come out of the house and was struggling to lift Emma out of the back of the estate car. She shrieked piercingly once or twice, and I almost covered my ears. Could it really hurt that much? I was appalled at the noise.

That little wretch Adam was still struggling in his car seat, and his screams were even louder than

Emma's. Lucinda had swung herself out of the driver's seat, and was standing next to Brian, holding a huge pair of crutches.

"Can you put those down and give me a hand?" Brian said to her. She looked hot and cross, and thrust the crutches at Sam, who had climbed out of the car and was watching with interest. He took the crutches from his mother and started trying to use them as stilts, jumping up on the hand-hold of one and pushing off with the other. Naturally he ended up on the gravel with the crutches on top of him, but had better sense than to yell as he crashed to the ground. One look at his mother's face told him that it wouldn't be wise to aggravate her further. His absurd antics had silenced the baby, who was staring at him solemnly and round-eyed. Even the sheepdog sat transfixed on the passenger seat.

Between them, Lucinda and Brian had managed to slide Emma into some kind of sitting position, her good leg hanging down over the tail of the estate car, and the plastered one sticking out stiffly.

"Bite on a rag, my darling," advised Brian, who was really very nice, and adored his daughter, holding out his handkerchief to Emma, who took one look at it and said "no thanks" in an offended way, forgetting to squeal for a minute.

It was better than a pantomime or a TV comedy, I decided, until I remembered that poor Emma really had no chance of doing anything at all for the rest of the holiday, trussed up in all that plaster, unable to move, let alone walk. I couldn't see that the crutches would be much use to her, either — they were almost as tall as she was.

With Lucinda on one side of her, and the smaller Brian on the other, Emma was carried through the back door. There was some confusion when they got there as to who was going first, resulting in Emma being swung round in a full circle before Brian was pushed in ahead and sideways on. The three of them disappeared, looking like the end of a Conga at a party. The fun seemed to be over as the door banged behind them. Only Adam was left, writhing in his car seat, straining at the harness, red in the face and yelling again as the sheepdog twisted round and began to lick at the tears which ran down his face. I was just thinking that it would be kind to go and rescue him, when Sam reappeared with Joanna, who was carrying the black kitten which she had found in the stable.

"I've got some stilts," he told her importantly, waving the crutches dangerously near her head. "Mum bought them for me in a toy shop."

Joanna watched him, impressed by the present. The kitten struggled free and made a dash for the stable.

"D'you want a go, Jo?" he asked, and thrust one of the crutches into her hands. "Hold this a sec.

Look," he said, "this is how you do it," and he
leapt into the air, hooking one foot over the hand-
hold again, and making a grab for the other crutch.
He swayed and Joanna backed away, and Sam
tumbled on to the concrete before I could catch
him. Luckily he didn't seem to be hurt, and he
jumped up quickly.

"You're not very good," said Joanna.

"I just need a bit more practice," retorted Sam.
"Anyway — bet you can't do it!"

"Bet I can," Joanna replied.

"Well, you're not going to, not just at the
moment," I told her firmly. "Go and feed the
pony again, and then we're going home. Here,
take these mints for Lorna."

Sam's eyes lit up at the sight of the sweets: "I'll
help you, Jo — wait a sec." He looked at me before
he followed her, and said, "Mum says the pony's
not safe. She says it's got to be sold."

"You're making it up," I said, horrified at this
bombshell. This was even worse news.

"I'm not — she told Emma in the car."

He left me staring at nothing while he ran after
Joanna, dragging the crutches behind him. In a
minute or so he clattered past me again, heading
for the house. His spare hand clutched something
which looked suspiciously like my tube of mints.
Joanna was staring after him with something like
admiration on her face.

"Isn't he lucky to have those stilts?" she said to me, waving to Sam as he banged noisily through the back door.

I couldn't reply. I crossed over to Lorna and leaned my head against her soft face. It was no use crying. She wasn't mine, and there was nothing I could do.

"Get on the bike," I said to Joanna, untying Brock from the gate. "There's nothing for us to do but go home."

SIX
My dream comes true

Our Easter eggs, which we were given the next morning, couldn't cheer me up much. I'd started the sponsored fast the night before, and had to starve myself until seven p.m. I was already ravenous just after breakfast, and couldn't raise any enthusiasm for hunting round the house for the tiny chocolate eggs that had been hidden. Joanna always found the most, because Jonathan and I couldn't be bothered to get down on our hands and knees to search. It made me feel ill to see her stuffing herself with chocolate when I couldn't have any.

It was no help at all to see my own large Easter egg in its glossy box, sitting tantalisingly on the dresser, waiting ... Was it a coincidence that it was Black Magic, I wondered? Or was it an omen?

I gazed at it; I could almost taste the chocolate hidden under the shiny red wrapping. The name leapt out at me: Black Magic, Black Magic!

"Like it, Becky?" Dad was asking. "I chose it for you, so save some for me tonight, unless you'd like me to open it for you now and help you out, as you can't have any?"

"Leave it alone, Dad. No-one's to touch it, especially the box. Understand?"

"All right, don't get aereated!"

"Well, you're so greedy! You'd eat it all as soon as my back was turned."

"Rubbish! How could you think anything like that about me? Anyway, what about it?" He was staring out of the window.

"What about what?"

"A sail, of course! Just the day for it! I've heard the forecast — 'sea area Plymouth, southwest three to four' — who's for a day out? It'll never be better."

I shuddered at the thought, and kept quiet.

"You go off and enjoy yourself, dear," Mum urged him. "We've all got other things to do today."

"Such as?" enquired Dad, looking surprised that anything could be more important or interesting than a day's sailing.

"What about you, Becky? Or Jon? Every chance missed is a chance lost for ever."

"No thanks, Dad," Jon and I both said together.

"What *are* you going to do, then? I hope you've

got something in mind."

"I'm going up to Emma's," I said quickly, more to keep him quiet than anything. Joanna joined in then: "You can't; she won't be able to do anything with that leg, and the pony's being sold anyway."

I scowled at her and wished her at the bottom of the sea. Why did she have to put her foot in it?

"You didn't tell me that," said Dad. "That's all right then — you're free to come sailing, aren't you?

"No!" I shouted. "No, no, no! When will you understand that I don't want to go sailing, I don't like sailing, I'll never like sailing! I only like horses, and if I can't go riding I don't know what I'll do!"

I heard myself shouting this out, with horror. It didn't sound like me at all. It sounded like some awful spoilt child. They were all staring at me. No-one said anything, and it seemed as if the room was still echoing with the sound of my shouting, even though there was silence. I rushed out then, into the garden, with the ever enthusiastic Brock at my heels, jumping up and barking with excitement at having someone who would run about with him. Little did he know that my spirits were at their lowest ebb, and a great black cloud was hovering over me, threatening to engulf me altogether in a storm of tears.

I ran up the hill and out of the top of the orchard into the wood, where I collapsed in a heap under a holly tree on a pile of dried prickly leaves. Brock

barked at me a few times, hoping it was some sort
of game, but then he set off into the undergrowth
and I could hear him snuffling about after an
imaginary rabbit.

I didn't stay under the holly tree for long, it was
too uncomfortable, and as soon as I heard the
sound of the outboard motor and knew that whoever was going sailing had gone, I sauntered down
into the house again, shamefaced.

Mum was sitting down with a cup of coffee and
a book. There was no sign of Jonathan or Joanna.
She looked up as I wandered in.

"There you are," she said unnecessarily. "I'm
glad you're all right."

"I'm all right ... sorry I was stupid." I leaned
against her for a minute, and she patted my arm. I
began to feel better.

"Would you believe it?" she asked. "Joanna said
she wanted to go sailing with Dad. He was so
pleased, and they've gone off together with a picnic
lunch. Thank goodness somebody wants to go
with him. Jonathan's getting his sails and things,
ready to go out on his own. So what about you?
Shall we go for a walk, or do some cooking?"

"Don't talk about food, Mum! Not today. If
you don't mind, I'd rather go off on my own.
There's somewhere I want to explore, and I'll take
Brock as Joanna's not here. I'll be quite all right,
and I've got to do *something*. I can't eat any lunch,

so I must get out and take my mind off food, and that Easter egg sitting there staring at me. It'll be even worse for Emma, I suppose. Poor thing, she won't be able to do anything except lie about and dream of Easter eggs and pasties and chips and cake and ice cream, and I'll bet that little brother of hers will be stuffing his chocolate right in front of her."

"Perhaps she'll give it up," said Mum.

"She can't—lots of people have given her money already."

"Is Lorna really being sold? You didn't say anything before."

"That's what Sam said. He said his Mum thought she wasn't safe."

"You don't want to take any notice of Sam. He's always making up stories, just to get attention. I'm sure Lucinda will tell you if it's true, so don't get too worried about it until you know for sure."

"I hope you're right, Mum, but I've got a hunch you're not. Anyway, I'll try what you suggested, and forget all about it—turn the clock back."

I knew just where I was going—to the ruined barn. Emma hadn't believed that I'd go there alone, but I knew from the very first sight of it that sooner or later I'd return. From the beginning it had a strange fascination for me, a magnetic pull. Now the moment was right, and I climbed the old church path through the bluebell wood, swinging my camera. I thought I might get some good shots of Brock in the sunlight.

The first flowers were showing already, stabs of deep blue beneath the oak trees. Brock was at my feet, but ran ahead at the top of the path to climb the ancient stone stile in his agile way and dash out into the short grass of the top field, hoping to see a rabbit. There were none in sight, though. They must have heard him coming.

I retraced the route of our Good Friday ride into what we called the muddy lane, but the other way round so that I didn't have to pass Emma's house. I knew I ought to call in to see how she was, but I couldn't face hearing first hand that Lorna was going to be sold. I'd pluck up courage to go and see her in a day or so, when I'd got used to the idea. I didn't want to face her Mum's disapproval, either. I knew it had all been my fault. I was beginning to feel a real martyr, taking the blame for Emma's broken leg, and also starving myself for a whole twenty-four hours for the sake of children who had nothing. I shouldn't feel sorry for myself, really, but I couldn't help how I felt. My stomach was beginning to make the most awful empty noises, complaining for food.

"Be quiet!" I commanded it sharply, and Brock looked up at me in surprise.

"Not you, Brock—just me talking to my stomach." I'd put him on the lead when we reached the road, and we ran together down the hill where Lorna and I had met the car, Brock jumping round and trying to snatch the lead in his mouth, his short legs hardly seeming to touch the ground, and turned into the top end of the lane.

Immediately the dogs from the farm hurled themselves across the derelict yard, starting up a deafening noise with their wild barking and the quacking and clucking of the startled ducks and hens. Three large white geese followed the dogs towards the gate, stretching out their necks, beaks wide, making menacing noises. I was glad to be on the other side of the farmyard gate. Where on earth were the people who lived there? There was no sign of anyone.

I ran on past, laughing at the dogs, but knowing I wouldn't have dared to pass if the gate hadn't been between us. I had to drag Brock with me — brave as ever, he would have taken on all the geese and dogs singlehanded without a second thought.

We arrived at the broken old gate where Emma and I had stopped to look at the ruined barn, or whatever it was. I climbed up again to get a better view, and sat precariously on the top rail. Brock rummaged happily about at my feet, and the sun was hot on my back. If it hadn't been for the gnawing hunger, I'd have felt really contented, the spot was so peaceful and sheltered. I could have stayed all day, just lying in the sun under the hedge at the edge of the field, especially if I'd had a grazing horse to watch.

There were no other buildings in sight, and no sounds now from the dogs at the farm back up the lane. Two wheeling buzzards circled and mewed plaintively above the old barn, and darting swiftly over the grass in the nearest field, several swallows flew low, probably the very first to arrive for the summer, winging their way in from the sea.

Twisting on the top of the wobbling gate to watch the buzzards circling above my head, I almost fell off, and felt my jeans tear as a jagged piece of wood caught them. Emma had been right not to climb it in her immaculate jodhpurs. I could just hear her:

"... don't want to get caught ... come on ... getting really hungry ..."

Hungry, hungry, hungry — the thought of food was driving me out of my mind. I began to feel very strange and lightheaded. Suddenly the blue sky began to press down on me and the overgrown grass spun away from under the gate, which wouldn't hold me any longer. In slow motion I was turning, turning, the world was upside down and I was spinning round it, or was it spinning round me ...? Flashes of blue and green and gold shot before my eyes and through my head, and as the earth slowed down and I lay back, pillowed by the long soft grass, I could hear the retreating

sound of Lorna's hooves as she trotted away up
the lane.

Did I only fall off the gate? I looked around
wonderingly. I felt as if I'd been on a long journey.
Well, let Emma go if she wanted to, I could explore
the barn. I got up shakily to my feet. My head
ached and it felt as if I'd wrenched my back when I
fell. Funny that Emma hadn't stayed to see if I was
all right . . . really strange.

I pushed my way through the spinney and past
the grove of sad elms which wouldn't come into
leaf this spring or any other. The ground beneath
them was littered with small dead twigs and
branches. A tangle of brambles barred my way
and I had to skirt round them to the end of the
building. There were no windows or doors at all
on this side, and several great cracks split the old
stone walls from the roof to the ground. The end
wall was covered with a luxuriant growth of ivy,
and the bramble thicket spread inwards as if protecting the walls from intruders. I tried the other,
shadowed end of the building, and slipped quickly
through between the damp end wall and a derelict
outhouse which had almost crumbled away into a
heap of stones.

Before stepping out of the shadow I looked round
the corner to the front of the barn, making sure it
was deserted before I ventured out.

Strangely unsurprised, I stepped out into a sunny

clean cobbled yard. Brock ran ahead of me, sniffing the air but not barking. The place was silent, but with the unmistakeable scent of horses, a warm and pungent smell, and then from somewhere inside the building I heard the rustling of straw and the muffled shuffling of hooves.

I savoured the excitement of the moment, gazing out over the panorama of fields and hedges, woods and valleys, which lay beyond, stretching away timelessly to distant blurred hills which merged softly with the hazy blue sky. There were no other buildings in sight at all. This one seemed to be on the edge of a wilderness.

I turned back to stare at the barn, shielding my eyes against the sun. Brock had disappeared through a pair of large green doors which were slightly ajar. I put my head inside and in the dim light saw that it was a coach-house, containing a farm cart loaded up with bracken, its woodwork and wheel spokes recently cleaned and rubbed to a shine. Alongside stood a delicate pony cart, with huge high wheels and sparkling paintwork. Next to the coach-house, a small single doorway, also open, led into a tack room, where harness and brasses gleamed on wooden pegs.

The gentle rustling sounds were closer now, and I held my breath as I pushed open the third and last door, set at right angles to the others and with a barred window above to let in air and light. I waited for my eyes to become accustomed to the gloom, hardly daring to search in the row of stalls which slowly materialised. They were empty — clean and swept — except for the end one, where rays of golden light from a high window illuminated a shining black horse, huge in his confined space, muscles rippling and head tossing, jerking against the restricting lead rope which held him fast.

It was the stallion, my Black Magic — it had to be. I forgot everything else, and crossed quickly to him, rubbing his neck and face with delight. He seemed to share my pleasure, and pranced a little on the fresh straw, straining at the lead rope. Outside the stall, a fine saddle hung, ready to use, polished and soft. The bridle hung from a wooden peg next to it.

I didn't hesitate, but slung the saddle carefully over Black Magic's back and fastened the girth. Somehow it all came naturally as if I'd been doing it for years. No more fumbling with buckles and doing things up wrong. With sure hands I put the bridle on, and I could sense his excitement matching mine as I hung up the head collar and led him out into the yard.

Brock had followed me all round the building while I'd been exploring, without a single bark. He was too interested in all the new smells and sensations to utter a sound, and now waited patiently while I tightened the girth and pulled down the stirrups. I mounted easily, as if there were springs in my legs. Black Magic danced about on the cobbles, his hooves making a ringing, echoing noise in the sheltered yard, and then we were away, first at a fast trot and then breaking into a canter, Brock following closely, ready for anything. The horse knew the way and I left him to find it. Meadows and ditches, woodland paths and wide moorland — all flew past beneath his flying, pounding hooves, and I rode as I had always known I could, effortlessly and in paradise.

Through all the days that followed, and the madcap rides we shared, I lost all sense of time. The world I lived in was peopled only by Black Magic and me, and the silent terrier running at our heels. Of Emma I saw nothing. I do remember being surprised that she hadn't been in touch, but in a way I was glad, because I didn't want to see anyone, and I wouldn't have shared Black Magic with anybody, even her. I needed nothing and nobody else, so deep was my involvement.

During the whole of this time, I can't remember ever seriously wondering who Black Magic belonged to. I believed he'd been left there for me, but by whom? I brushed the question aside, refusing to think about it. Someone else other than me came and went. I knew that by the way things were moved — buckets and brushes, tack and straw. I soon took on the feeding and grooming. It never occurred to me not to do it. And the mucking-out was a pleasure, not a chore. I talked to my horse while I worked, and he answered in his way, nudging me with his strong, heavy head as I moved round him. But I never saw anybody else at the stable. The farm cart and the pony trap didn't move, although sometimes the scent of beeswax told me that someone had been there ahead of me, polishing tack or woodwork and rubbing up the horseshoes which hung over the door. I was there early every day and left only as dusk fell, but I was always alone.

Days passed in a blur of happiness. Time went by unnoticed. Black Magic and I were as one, whether stepping carefully through the first blue-bells in a sun-speckled copse, or galloping wildly across the open heather-clad moor, he read my thoughts and wishes. I hardly needed to use my legs or hands — there was a wonderful feeling of one-ness between us: security and exhilaration mingled to forge a perfect team. We could have won any race, excelled at any show, travelled any distance. Anything and everything was possible, success was certain.

Once I took him down to the river at low water, and he splashed through the shallow channel to the wide, golden sand flats in the dry river bed. There were no quicksands that day, as we galloped from one end to the other, his hooves kicking up the sand behind him, and showering me with cold water as he plunged through the shallow pools and the wind caught the spray and flung it high in the air. As the sandy strip narrowed and we turned for the gallop back, the herons nesting in their lofty dead tree heaved themselves clumsily into the air and glided towards us, croaking angrily at being disturbed. I waved as we left them behind, hooves pounding, and the river bed vibrating as we gathered speed.

"Yoohoo," I yelled, looking over to my house, right on the edge of the muddy flats beyond the sand, long and white, protected by the dense woodland behind. "Halloooo Mummmmmm," I called, into the wind, waving at nothing as we streaked onwards and out of sight of the house and anyone who had been watching.

But when I asked them afterwards, no-one had seen anything, or heard me shout. And I only took him there once. At least I can remember it all and re-live it, if I can bear to.

Subconsciously I must have known it couldn't last, that it would come to an end. It was too perfect to stay the same for ever. But I couldn't have believed that it would end the way it did, so suddenly, finished, ended, gone for ever. Perhaps someone, somewhere, had decided I'd had more than my fair share of luck.

The last day began like any of the other perfect

days. I groomed Black Magic until his coat shone and reflected like polished ebony. I could almost see my face in his neck, which felt like finest velvet. His mane and tail were soft to my touch after all the brushing and combing I gave them. I oiled his hooves and made sure his feet were free from stones before turning my attention to the tack. The leather was already gleaming and smelling pungent with polish, but I did it all again just because I wanted to. He looked magnificent: I was so proud of him, and he was mine.

I banished the niggling voice that reminded me he wasn't, and he never would be. This was the day to photograph him. I would take a portrait and have it enlarged and mounted on my bedroom wall. That way he would be with me all the time.

I led him out, fully tacked up, into the sunny still yard. The only sounds were of larks soaring into a perfect blue and cloudless sky, and the distant murmuring of wood pigeons. The day was fresh and pure, and he and I lifted our faces to sniff the air. He stood motionless and gleaming, like a bronzed statue, the sun gilding his shining coat, while I fetched the camera from the tack room and took several photos. Brock as usual was a silent onlooker, basking on the warmth of the cobbles with his head on his paws, eyes alert and ears cocked, ready for the ride.

Finally I was satisfied with my photos, and left

the camera on a ledge inside the stable door.

I swung myself easily into the saddle, and felt Black Magic's eagerness matching my own. With a final pat to his muscular neck, I turned him towards the open country, only to feel him hesitate and stiffen beneath me. For once he didn't respond to my hands and voice, but instead he snorted and tossed his head and took several steps backwards. Immediately alarmed, I looked about me, and to my dismay saw a figure I recognised emerging from the dark passageway at the side of the building. I had seen him once before, holding Lorna, with that peculiar possessive look on his face, after Emma's fall.

"No, no!" I shouted frantically, trying to turn Black Magic away, as the man came towards us with that same greedy look on his brown, lined face. "No, please, no!"

And Black Magic continued his retreat as the man came relentlessly on. I felt the powerful muscles tense, and knew that for the first and only time he was going to rear and throw me off. I waited for it — it seemed for ever — and then as if in slow motion I flew up and away from him, and fell endlessly, and into a black abyss.

SEVEN
The end of the dream

Brock woke me with his persistent nagging bark. I opened my eyes to stare at him in surprise, he had been silent for so long.

I expected my head to hurt badly after a fall like that one—surely some part of me would be broken? But I felt all right, just a little dizzy and strange in the head. If only Brock would shut up.

It was so hot, and the sun so dazzling. I squinted up from where I lay against the grassy bank. Someone was leaning over the gate. An angry face moved, shouting:

"Here you! You've no business there! Come on out—it's private! You're trespassing!" The furious voice went on and on: "You can't go wandering round other folks' property just when you feel like it! The very idea, sunbathing in my field! I'll give you sunbathing!" He waved a stick at me over the gate, and Brock's bark rose to a hysterical note. "And get your dog out of here before I set mine on it!"

I thought he'd never stop ... but why was I lying by the gate? I must have hit the cobbles with a real crack—I could remember flying through the air, and the blackness ... but I'd been in the yard, so how had I got here? It didn't make sense; I couldn't think, it was crazy.

Brock was letting the man have the full treatment—ears back, teeth bared, fur standing up along his back, and a menacing growl. An angry Jack Russell is a frightening sight, but the man was still muttering away at me. I didn't like the look of him any more than Brock did: a battered and green-mouldy trilby was squashed on top of the round red face, and he seemed to be dressed in sacking—one sack round his shoulders, partly covering a dirty, collarless shirt stretched across a bulging stomach, and another worn apron-like round his waist, tied up with orange binder twine, over muddy trousers and even muddier heavy boots. I decided it was probably the farmer from the mucky old place with the dogs and chickens up the lane.

I got up with as much dignity as I could manage, and tried to stare confidently at him, without success, as I found my legs were very wobbly. I made a grab at Brock, who evaded me and made another dive for the farmer's ankles in between barks.

"Come here, you stupid dog," I snapped at him, feeling flustered.

"You want to train him better than that," the man said contemptuously. "He'll get into trouble before long." And he aimed a deft kick at the irritating little animal, which would have hurt if it had caught him in the ribs where it was intended to.

I fought back the temptation to give him a piece of my mind about cruelty to animals, and instead made a dive for Brock, catching him by the tail, which was my last resort when he was in a scrap. I'd read somewhere that if you pulled him away by the tail, he couldn't reach round to bite you. I hoped that whoever had written that had been right. I managed to get him on the lead, which I found to my surprise in my pocket.

I was wondering how to get back to the stable yard; I knew I had to go back for something ... my camera! That was it, my camera. But first I had to persuade this bad-tempered man.

"I've left something in the stable; you don't mind if I fetch it, do you?" I had to be polite or he might not let me go. "I'm sorry if I've been trespassing — I didn't realise."

"You've been down to the old barn as well, have you? Well, you've no right to go there. No-one goes there. It's all private. I could have you prosecuted for wilful damage if you've touched anything."

"Please, it's just my camera that I've left there. I must go and get it." With that I tugged at Brock and ran down through the spinney and past the dead elms. I glanced back from there to see the farmer struggling with the twine that held the gate closed. He was going to come after me to see that I hadn't done any damage. I had to be quick.

I slipped round the end of the coach-house and into the yard, and stopped dead. The smooth cobbles were gone — now they were cracked and choked with weeds. Beyond, instead of open wide spaces and tantalising inviting countryside, were choking brambles and creeping ivy covering broken walls, and plain fields and trees and the everyday valley that I recognised.

I whirled round to stare at the building: the doors to the coach-house were gone, a gaping space inside held nothing at all. The clean, white-washed walls had turned green and black with decay and mould. The tack-room door was still there, but hanging off the top hinge and stuck in the doorway. I ran to look inside, but it was dark and smelt of damp. The last door to the stable was closed and tied up with orange binder twine. I couldn't bring myself to go near it.

I had known it would end, but this was too final. I felt as if it was the end of the world.

The farmer had caught me up. Brock was strangely quiet again, and lying down in his favourite sunny corner, unaware of any change or of my dismay.

"Where is it, then?" the man was asking.

I looked at him blankly, thinking of something else.

"The camera. Find it quickly and then be off, and don't come back. I might not be so nice next time." He waved his stick at me again, and I backed away towards the stable door. I untied the twine and stepped inside, without looking round. I could still sense the unmistakeable presence of the horse, but he wasn't there any more, I knew. The camera was on the shelf where I had left it, just inside the door. But the shelf was thick with dust. It had been spotless before — I'd cleaned it myself. A deep sense of unease gripped me then, as if I was being watched by someone unseen.

I didn't want the stable to be changed. I wanted it to stay the way it had been for ever. I stepped quietly outside, tying up the door behind me, shutting in my memories. Longing to be away from the place now, I caught hold of Brock's lead and ran out of the yard without a backward look at the staring farmer, holding tightly to the precious camera, and almost tripping on the rough cobbled remains that had so recently rung happily to the sound of powerful horseshoes.

I walked home in a daze, oblivious to the things I usually noticed: birds, wild flowers, trees, patterns of clouds. It could have rained or shone, snowed or thundered. I was neither hot nor cold, wet nor dry, awake nor dreaming. I didn't understand what had happened. One moment I was one person, the next moment everything had changed and I was different. It seemed so final, finished. Brock and my own legs led me home, and as I walked into the house I felt like a stranger.

"You look better, Becky," Mum said surprisingly when she saw me. "The walk must have done you good. Did you do what I suggested and turn back the clock and forget about things? Much the best thing to do when you feel miserable. You haven't been out too long, either, so you can have a nice afternoon at home. You'll be really ravenous by supper time, I'm sure. Shame you can't have any Easter cake for tea, but you can have some tomorrow. We're having a specially nice meal to-night as a treat for you — I'm making a lovely pudding. I see you took the camera. Did you get some good snaps?" She rambled on . . .

"Emma phoned. She wants to speak to you when you have time to phone her. I asked if she was fasting as well, but she said she didn't do it, like you suspected. She sounded really fed up — she can't do anything at all with her leg all plastered. I think she's relying on you to cheer her up."

I stared at her — "Emma? Of course, her leg. But it must be getting better by now. I'd forgotten all about it ..."

It was Mum's turn to stare at me: "Whatever do you mean? She only did it yesterday. It'll be weeks before she can walk properly. Surely you knew that? What a peculiar thing to say, Becky." She studied me more closely: "Where have you been this morning? Have you been lying in the sun? Your eyes look funny. Do you feel all right?"

I suddenly gave up, and collapsed on to the kitchen chair, my head in my hands. "No, I don't feel all right. I'll never feel all right again. Everything's gone wrong." I tried, but I couldn't prevent the tears from dripping through my fingers on to the floor. Brock licked them up, and I had to laugh at that. But I couldn't explain to anyone what had happened. I couldn't even understand it myself. I knew it was all real, not just a dream, but I'd never convince anyone else of that.

"Did you lie in the sun? Is that it?" Mum sounded concerned. "I thought you looked better, but something must be the matter. Is it just that you're hungry? You'd better give up this silly fasting and have a sandwich. It can't be doing you any good to go without food."

"I can't give it up now." I was beginning to remember things again. "What time is it?"

"Three o'clock."

"So how much longer have I got?"

"Four hours, of course."

"Only four hours — that's nothing. I'll be all right in a minute. It must be because I fell off the gate." But had I fallen off the gate? I didn't really know.

Mum was worried then: "When? Which gate? Did you hurt yourself? Bang your head? Let me look at you." She studied my face and felt my head for bumps. "You'd better go and lie down on your bed. I'll bring you a cup of tea." Mum's cure for all ills. She pushed me off to bed, and burying my head thankfully into the darkness under the bedclothes, I drifted away on the end of my dream, if dream it was, into a deep and empty sleep.

The phone woke me, ringing shrilly and insistently, on and on until I couldn't ignore it any longer. Where was everyone? Why did it have to be me? I heaved myself out of bed and slumped into the hall, feeling dreadful: headachy and sick. "Hello?" I managed weakly.

"Ah, Becky," a brisk voice answered. "I was just beginning to think you were all out."

"I was," I mumbled, "absolutely out."

"What was that? Oh never mind. It's Lucinda here." As if I hadn't recognised her, booming like a trombone down the line.

"How are you, dear?" she asked as an afterthought.

"Just about starving," I replied. "How's Emma?"

"Not too good, that's why I'm phoning. I'm sorry to tell you — (and I knew what was coming) — we've decided that Lorna has to go. We can't risk Emma out on an unreliable pony."

"But . . ." I began.

"No buts, dear, please. We've told her our decision and she's accepted it. She's going to have a new bike instead and maybe a guinea pig or a rabbit."

I raised my eyes to heaven, and my spirits sank to the floor. There was nothing I could say in answer to that. She went on: "However . . . until we can sell Lorna she'll have to be exercised, and of course Emma can't even walk about until she gets used to her crutches, and she won't try them at the moment, goodness knows why. So we're hoping that, if you haven't anything else to do, you'll be free at least for the rest of the holidays to give Lorna a short ride each day, and do the chores, of course."

Of course, I thought.

"Are you sure she's safe for *me* to ride?" I enquired with as much sarcasm as I dared, but fortunately Lucinda was talking again and didn't notice. "Shall we expect you tomorrow, then? Any time will do, as long as it's not too late. We must keep Lorna looking smart in case anyone wants to come and view, mustn't we? It would be so helpful if you could take over completely. Emma's quite helpless, and the boys aren't exactly easy, and Brian's not a lot of use one way and another ..." Her voice tailed off, and suddenly I was sorry for her. Despite her manner, she must have had an awful shock about Emma, and it was true that Brian wasn't exactly a practical kind of man ... I wished she wouldn't refer to Lorna like a piece of property, though, instead of a living breathing pony, with feelings.

"Don't worry," I forced myself to say a bit more pleasantly. "I'll be over tomorrow and help with anything I can. Tell Emma I'll see her then."

"You are a good girl. I knew I could depend on you. Bye now." And she rang off, leaving me wondering what I'd let myself in for, especially if it took them ages to sell poor Lorna. If she'd asked me yesterday I'd have jumped at the chance. I'd been so upset when Sam told me that Lorna was going to be sold. Now it didn't seem to matter so much, and dear old unexciting Lorna didn't seem quite so special. Who on earth could think she wasn't reliable? She must be the most reliable pony in the world.

Four o'clock: my stomach was making the most alarming noises, and the Easter eggs — even my Black Magic one — watched me smugly from where they were lined up on the dresser. I noticed that Joanna's was almost finished. It seemed weeks ago that she had gone off sailing with Dad.

I was going mad with the thought of food — or the lack of it — and in the end I had to go outside to watch for Dad's return, to get away from the temptation of raiding the kitchen. Looking out over the river I could see the red sails of Jonathan's dinghy as it scudded about in the breeze — good enough for a photo. I fetched my camera and finished up the film with a couple of shots of the river and the contrasting red sails, but after that there didn't seem anything else to do.

Jonathan sailed over and ran the little boat onto the shingle in front of the house. "Want to come for a quick burn? It's ace today. You'd enjoy it." Why not, I thought, to my own surprise and even more to his.

We tacked up the river for a bit and then ran down past the house, which looked spectacular as always, bathed in sunlight and protected in its isolation by the surrounding trees. The little dinghy was travelling fast, despite our combined weights, and the house grew smaller in the distance. We crossed the widest part of the river, heading off towards the old boathouse, which looked sadder and more derelict then ever.

"Want to land?" asked Jonathan, looking at me. I shook my head. I hadn't been there since Christmas, and I still couldn't bring myself to go ashore. I wanted to forget that particular adventure.

"Take the helm, then," he said, standing up and making the boat rock precariously. Without waiting for me to agree or otherwise, we had somehow changed places and I found myself with the tiller in my hand.

"Gybe-o," he instructed me, pulling my hand on the tiller, and the little boat skidded away in the direction of the tiny creek where all our neighbours lived. Only a handful of them, the Fieldings and a few others, just a collection of cottages and gardens on the edge of the water. The sun streamed down on us as we sped across the river, Jonathan holding on to the jib sheet, leaning out and grinning with pleasure. I realised with amazement that I was enjoying myself. It was almost like galloping on Black Magic, the same sensation of speed and freedom. Perhaps there was something in this sailing business after all. Even the emptiness inside me seemed to have been settled by the motion of the boat. The wind pulled my hair away from my face and showers of spray fell refreshingly on my bare arms — strange to think that in a few hours this would all be firm dry sand where people could walk or ride, just as I had done on Black Magic. But when? Yesterday, last week, or sometime in the future? Or even sometime in the past? It was a sobering thought. I was fantasising again — mustn't do it.

I shook myself back to reality as Jonathan shouted

"Ready about," and pushed my tiller hand away. A brief lull and a flap of the red sails and we were dashing away in the opposite direction, up the main river heading for a waterside church, the tower tall and grey, seeming to watch over this wide and peaceful stretch of the river. We landed there on the shingle beach and wandered among the grey gravestones clustered in the grassy churchyard next to the water.

In the distance Jon spotted Dad and Joanna returning in the grey dinghy. We raced home, trying to catch them up, but the engine won and they were already ashore, faces flushed and hair wild — a sure sign that they had been out to sea — when we eventually arrived. Dad looked amazed to see me sailing with Jon.

"You must come with me next time, Becky. It's marvellous out at sea — another world."

"Maybe, Dad, maybe. I'm not promising anything. Anyway, the only thing I'm interested in now is food. How much longer have I got to wait?"

"Is it teatime?" Joanna asked. "We only had biscuits on the boat and I'm starving. Mum! Mum!" She rushed inside, shedding her life jacket and boots and oilskin on the way, with Brock at her heels barking a welcome. Drifting out of the kitchen were delicious cooking smells which told me what I was waiting for. I knew it was going to be chicken, roast potatoes, roast parsnips, sprouts and gravy, followed by chocolate sponge pudding and custard—and that was without going into the kitchen to look!

"It's only five, Becky." Dad was looking at his watch. "Two hours to go." I groaned. The afternoon seemed endless, the time dragged like a lifetime. I'd never make it.

But I did. The magic hour of seven o'clock arrived, and exactly on the second I broke into my Black Magic Easter egg, running my fingers lovingly over the embossed name on the red and gold box. Jon spoilt the moment for me, as only he could. As I savoured the taste of the first mouthful, he glanced at me slyly: "Has it occurred to you that the starving children in Ethiopia have never tasted chocolate, and that the cost of that egg would feed one family for a month?" I was furious with him, because the dark rich chocolate seemed to turn sour in my mouth, but even he couldn't spoil the supper I had. I felt I'd deserved it, whatever he thought about the chocolate.

Mum heaped food on my plate, and I filled myself to bursting point. "More, Mum, please more," I begged after my second helping of pudding, but there was none left, so I scraped the pudding bowl and the custard jug of every last scrap, and still felt hungry. Jon passed me the remains of his Easter egg. "Here, I'm not so keen on chocolate these days — you can finish this up."

"No thanks, not after what you said earlier."

"Don't be stupid — I was only joking."

"Well, I didn't think it was funny."

Dad put out his hand for the egg: "Funny person not liking chocolate. I'll do you a favour and finish it. Nobody bought me one." Jon's egg soon vanished. We always said Dad was a chocoholic.

"I'll never do that again," I vowed. "It's not worth it. In fact, the day's been a nightmare."

"Of course it's worth it," Mum replied. "You've earned £5 for charity, that must be worthwhile."

But that wasn't important any more. I was thinking that my life would never be the same again, after a glimpse into my perfect world.

EIGHT
The photograph

The following morning I took the film out of my camera and posted it on my way to Emma's. I hoped the prints would come back quickly. At the letter box I made a wish that they would answer some questions for me. I just hoped they wouldn't all be blanks, with an irritating note of advice from the printers. All I could do was to wait.

I found Emma lying on the settee, still in her dressing gown and nightshirt, watching TV.

"There's nothing else to do," she said defensively. "Look at my leg, like a huge tree trunk — I can't move an inch."

Sam had decorated the white plaster with felt pen designs and red and blue hand prints. It looked amazing, but Emma's face was downcast.

"What can I do?" she appealed to me. "I'm going

to be stuck here for weeks, almost paralysed."

"I'll bring you some books tomorrow," I replied unimaginatively. I really couldn't think of anything else she could do just lying there. "I'm going out to see to Lorna now. I'll come back and tell you how I get on later."

"OK," she replied without much interest. Sam came pelting in then, in full cry after the kitten, who leapt over the top of Emma and hid under the settee. Sam was just about to follow it, but I grabbed him just in time. Emma had already opened her mouth to yell, but she closed it again, looking at me helplessly as I steered Sam away by the collar. "Come on, Superman!" I said. "You can help me with the stable." He wriggled and protested all the way out into the yard and looked offended when I put a fork into his hands.

"Clean out the stable," I told him sternly. "Put all the dirty straw and dung in the wheelbarrow and tip it onto the heap. When you've done that, I'll tell you what to do next." To my surprise he gave me one resentful look and then began to work. Good, I thought—that's a start. I shan't have to do everything myself if I play my cards right. Perhaps I was being a bit hard on him—he was only six.

Lorna was easy to catch and groom, and before long the stable was clean, the pony tacked up, and I was ready for my ride.

"When I get back, Sam, we'll clean the tack," I announced. Might as well make myself completely unpopular while I was about it, I decided. "And that's how it's going to be every day," I continued. "And—if you help me each time, *each* time, mind, I'll give you a reward at the end of the week."

His face brightened: "What? What will you give me?"

"I'll think of something really special."

"Will it cost a lot?"

"Probably it won't cost anything." He looked doubtful. "How can it be really special and not cost anything? You're making it up. I don't believe you'll give me anything at all."

"Yes, I will, I promise. And I always keep promises."

"Not everyone does. Emma doesn't. She promised me a ride and I never got one."

"Then when I get back you can have a ride— today—just a short one."

I left him with some relief, and took Lorna for a gentle amble round the lanes, once or twice venturing into a trot on the grass verge, lost in thought, alone but not lonely. It was good to be riding again. It felt as if an age had passed since Black Magic and I had galloped together all over the countryside. Lorna was such an easy ride—all I had to do was to sit there dreaming. It was hardly riding at all. She took me back to Emma's without me telling her which way to go. I suddenly found we were there, and Lorna was clattering into the yard. Goodness knows which way we'd gone. I'd been miles away in some other place with some other horse.

"Becky! Becky!" Sam was yelling at me. "It's my turn now. Give me your hat!" He took it out of my hand and put it on his small head — it covered his eyes!

"Come here, idiot." I took it off him, and we found a smaller one hanging on a peg. Lucinda came bustling out of the side door of the house, the baby on her hip. He was crying as usual, and the huge hairy dog was leaping up at him, making matters worse.

"Becky! Becky! When you've given Sam his ride, can you come in and amuse Emma for a bit? I've got to go shopping now. I'll leave Adam in his pram in the garden. If he cries, his bottle's ready in the kitchen, but you'll have to heat it. I don't suppose he'll be any trouble to you, though." She hurried inside again with the yelling baby and barking dog, leaving me staring after her.

Sam was nagging at me to give him a leg up. It took an age for him to have a ride round the field because he kept asking questions and demanding to go round again, and again, and in the end I had to almost drag him off Lorna, pretending that she was tired. She wasn't, of course: she went so slowly that she couldn't possibly be tired.

I conveniently forgot about cleaning the tack. I could get Sam to do that tomorrow. I could hear Adam wailing from the garden, so I went out to the pram under the trees and picked him up awkwardly. I thought this was carrying friendship a bit far, I must admit. Strangely enough he stopped crying after a minute or two, so I took him in to Emma, who didn't look any more pleased with life than she had earlier.

"Let's have a milk shake, Becky. You can do it. Sam'll show you where everything is." I handed her the baby but she waved him away with irritation, making a face and wrinkling her nose. "I don't want him — he's smelly and damp. You'll have to walk about with him under one arm like Mum does, unless you want to change his nappy, of course. Do get me a milk shake, I'm so thirsty, and some peanut butter sandwiches — I'm starving."

Funnily enough, the baby wasn't wet and smelly at all, but quite nice and warm and cuddly. His soft hair reminded me of Lorna's warm neck. I made Sam get the milk shakes while I held the baby on my lap. Sam obviously knew his way round the kitchen, but he did everything in a furtive way, as if he wasn't supposed to touch anything. After a bit he relaxed and chatted to me, and I decided that he was really quite sensible, and the baby was gorgeous. I began to enjoy myself, and that's how it continued for the next week — riding Lorna each morning and leaving Sam to do the stable work. It was hard for him, being so young, but he struggled on with it, and afterwards he rode on Lorna in the field, and then I looked after the baby while I chatted to Emma over our lunch. Lucinda liked to go shopping each day, or to some committee meeting or coffee morning, so we had the place to ourselves. Brian was usually off doing some deal or other, making money, I supposed.

I don't know what Mum would have thought of our lunches — peanut butter sandwiches, or heaps of toast with whatever Sam could find in the larder, or bowls of cereal with ice cream. Emma never dressed or even seemed to move. She just lay on the settee while I came and went. I don't think anyone bothered about her except me. Sometimes she wanted to talk and sometimes not. She watched a lot of television and glanced through a lot of magazines. Lucinda brought her a new one every time she went shopping. It seemed to me that she was wasting time — she could have tried the crutches and got out into the garden, or she could have read lots of really good books. But she wouldn't. The only time she was really cheerful was when she was telling me about the new bike she'd been promised, and the pets she was going to keep in a cage when she was better. She didn't ask about Lorna at all, and always interrupted me when I started to tell her about my ride.

On the Friday Sam wanted to know what I was going to give him as a reward for helping with the pony. I racked my brains and in the end told him I'd definitely tell him the next day, and that it would be a surprise. A surprise to me as well, because at that time I had no idea what I could give him.

But Saturday morning brought another disappointment. My new-found contentment was shattered by the sight of Sam's tear-stained face as he waited for me at the gate, and by his first words: "Lorna's going tomorrow. Dad's sold her." His normally perky face was downcast and sad. "I won't be able to ride any more, will I? And you won't be coming again, will you?" He watched me anxiously as I digested the bad news. I'd known it was coming, I suppose, but not as soon as this.

The holidays had been a series of ups and downs. Nothing had gone to plan. One moment I'd been on a high note, the next plunged into gloom. I wondered if life was always going to be like that. I answered him briskly to keep his mind off the news: "Never mind (I *hated* it when people said that to me), don't moan about it. It's not as bad as all that (but of course it was). I've brought something for you, but you can't have it until the tack's cleaned. We don't want the new owners to think we haven't looked after her."

Brian emerged from the side door and paid one of his rare visits to the yard, staying well away from Lorna, even though she stood as placidly as ever while I saddled her up. He looked a bit embarrassed, I thought, as he leaned against the wall watching. Eventually he came out with what he wanted to say: "I'm afraid this is your last ride, Becky. Someone's offered me a good price for the pony, one that I can't refuse. She's going tomorrow. I'm sure she'll have a good home, and she's no use to us if Emma's not going to ride her again, is she? Don't you think it's the right thing to do? We couldn't keep her, could we?"

If he was waiting for me to agree with him, he was disappointed. I just shrugged my shoulders and carried on getting Lorna ready. I wondered how anyone could part with a pony so casually, here one week and gone the next, as if she was a pair of shoes that had gone out of fashion, or a toy that a child had got tired of. If Lorna had been my pony I'd never have parted with her. She would have been one of the family, not something to be cast aside the moment something went slightly wrong.

I did say, "What about Sam?" Brian looked puzzled. "What about Sam?" he echoed enquiringly.

"Sam likes riding and he's getting quite good. He'll miss it when Lorna's gone."

"Sam's only six. He doesn't know what he likes

yet. We can't keep a pony for a six-year-old, especially if there's any risk of another accident. Anyway, he's got his bike and plenty of other toys."

After that, I just couldn't bring myself to say any more, but I wondered why they'd been happy for me to ride if they thought it was such a risk. There didn't seem to be any point in arguing, especially when Brian added, "I've got the cheque for her. It came this morning. I've made a nice profit, too, so she hasn't cost me anything. Emma can have her new bike out of it without it costing me a penny."

I mounted quickly, and trotted off, furious. But it wasn't any use, he didn't realise how I felt. It was just a waste of time getting upset and spoiling my last ride. My last ride! I couldn't believe it was happening, and Lorna felt somehow more lively and ready than usual. I decided to go further afield and headed for the narrow lane where Emma and I had ridden on the very first day of the holidays. It was the same sort of day, and we trotted briskly along between scented hedgerows sprinkled with early bluebells and red campion.

Memories of my rides with Black Magic came flooding back as I gazed over the hedges into the valley beyond. But this wasn't a magic day — everything was too familiar. Even so I held my breath as we passed the broken-down gate leading to the old barn, half anticipating and half hoping that some sign would lead me back into that other world of make-believe. For I was certain that it was make-believe now. Life was too ordered and ordinary for things like that to happen except in dreams.

The barn slept peacefully in the morning sun, protected and sheltered by its surrounding trees and creeping brambles. The only sounds were the drone of a bee sampling the spring sunshine, and the occasional plaintive call from the lambs in the valley. No sound of stamping eager hooves or jingling bridle from the hidden stable yard. Nothing stirred except a swallow swooping low over the lush field. I broke the spell by urging Lorna on into a steady canter, with a final look backwards at the barn.

Imagination and bright sunlight play strange tricks. I could have sworn there was a figure standing by the gate, a brown, wizened gnome of a man, the same acquisitive expression on his face that I had seen before. He wanted Lorna, I could see that much. He'd taken Black Magic from me, and now he wanted Lorna as well. I kicked her on in a panic to get away from those searching possessive eyes, and when I turned again he had gone, disappeared in the same way as when I'd met him in the bottom lane when I was looking for Lorna.

I blinked, and blamed the slanting sunshine for what I'd seen, or more likely, imagined.

I was trembling, and afraid I'd meet the grumpy

old farmer. That would be the final straw, and
would really ruin my last ride, but although the
dogs rushed out to the farmyard gate and the fowls
and geese made a terrible cackle and quacking,
there was no sign of human life in the yard. I
decided never to go that way again. It wasn't likely
that I would anyway, without a pony to ride.
Weird things happened along there, the strangest
feelings took possession of me, even though Lorna
sailed along placidly with no sign of nerves at all.
Surely that was reason enough to convince me that
it was all imagination on my part? The pony would
soon have sensed if anything was wrong or if she
or I were in any danger.

I patted her neck and talked to her gently, remembering that the next day she would be gone.
Brian hadn't said who she was going to. I hoped
he'd found out something about the people before
agreeing to part with her. You couldn't be too
careful about finding a good home for a horse. I
decided not to spend any time with Emma that
day. I couldn't understand her negative attitude to
Lorna. I was sure her parents wouldn't have sold
the pony if Emma had protested enough. To me it
was unbelievable.

Regretfully I walked Lorna slowly back to the
yard, highly aware of the creaking leather and the
warm back beneath me, the pricked ears which
flickered round when I spoke, the twitching tail

and the clopping hooves. There seemed nothing to look forward to now, nothing in prospect except school at the end of the week. It was a dismal outlook, and I felt deeply depressed as we turned into the yard.

Sam was waiting, looking dejected, and I rumpled his dark hair as I dismounted. He held Lorna for me while I found the parcel I had brought up for him, as his reward for helping me out all week. It was more than that, really, as his face told me when he opened his present—I had given him the clock radio that Denis and Dorothy had bought for me at Christmas. Somehow I wanted this parting with Lorna, and Sam, to hurt—and it did. I should remember how it felt to give away something that was precious to me. It made me all the more angry with Lucinda and Brian, but I was happy to see Sam's delight: "Wow! Brilliant, Becky. Thanks a million. Just what I've always wanted, but Dad said I was too young for a radio. He can't say anything now you've given me this. And a clock as well!"

For the moment his disappointment was forgotten, also his last ride. I didn't remind him, which wasn't fair, I know, but I just couldn't face the final circuit of the field. I just wanted to get away. I hung up the tack and turned Lorna out, and without even waiting to watch her roll, and without a backward look, I escaped, leaving the sounds of pop music fading behind me as Sam sat happily on a straw bale, fiddling with the radio.

I took the long way home, crossing the fields that overlooked the river, a panorama stretching as far as I could see, the river winding away through woods and towards distant hills. Cottages were dotted about below me: signs of life, people working in their gardens, smoke rising from cottage chimneys, Jonathan's red sails crossing and recrossing the river, yachts swaying gently at their moorings, flocks of white seagulls swooping down to the water, crows and buzzards wheeling above. All so familiar, and yet not what I wanted.

I dropped down through the steep fields and into the pathway leading to the creek. A small white hurricane hurtled up to meet me from the shoreline — Brock, followed closely by Joanna, rosy-faced and hot from running. "Becky! Becky!" she shouted. "Your films have arrived! I collected them from the letter box!"

My heart skipped at least one beat. "Where are they? What have you done with them?" I asked, as we met at the bottom of the path.

"I took them home; I didn't know where you were," she explained.

"Come on," I said, grasping her warm hand, but she tugged in the other direction.

"No. I want to go on up here; it won't take long." But I couldn't wait any longer to see my photos. Impatiently I pulled her the way I wanted to go, and she had to follow, protesting all the way. Mrs Hope, who lived in the first cottage we came to, had heard us and was waiting: "Coming in, dears? I've got fresh buns just out of the oven, just ready for visitors."

"No thanks, Mrs Hope, I've got to rush home," I called without stopping.

"But, Becky . . . " Joanna tried to say something but I hurried her on.

Further along the lane we were delayed by a gaggle of assorted dogs who had heard Brock and ran out to meet him. These were his friends, and they circled him in an energetic way, barking and sniffing and waving their tails.

"Come here, you horrors!" a faceless voice roared from behind the hedge. In the scramble that followed I managed to snatch Brock and escape, pulling Joanna away, protesting, from the boisterous and noisy collection of dogs.

It was just our luck that Dorothy Fielding had heard the uproar and spotted us coming past. She came to look over her fence, and I know I blushed red, remembering that I had given away her present. She wouldn't find out, but I still felt guilty.

"Come in, Becky dear, and have a cup of coffee. Denis and I have just put the chairs out. It's quite sheltered in the garden. I haven't seen you for ages. It's time we had a chat. Are you enjoying your holidays? And Joanna, what a big girl you're getting, aren't you? Really growing up."

Joanna scowled. Dorothy reached over and ruffled her hair with a little laugh. "What a funny little thing," she said, making matters worse. It was Joanna's turn to tug at my hand, backing away. "Come on, Becky, come on."

"Becky's coming in for a cup of coffee," Dorothy said firmly. "Aren't you, dear?"

"Well, I'm not," Joanna pronounced equally firmly and began to walk on towards the start of the footpath which led through the woods to our house. I looked at Dorothy with embarrassment, and said apologetically, "Really she ought not to walk home alone, and I have got something that I want to do. I could come tomorrow instead, if that's all right. I've nothing else to do." It wasn't true that Joanna couldn't walk home alone, but I couldn't face Dorothy or Denis asking me if the radio was working properly or something like that. I wouldn't have known what to say. By the next day I would have thought out my reply.

Dorothy looked a little surprised: "Tomorrow then, and you can tell me all about school." I sighed. Why did adults always think you wanted to talk about school, especially in the holidays when it was the last thing you wanted to be re-minded of. "All right, that'll be nice," I answered, wondering why it was impossible to tell the truth sometimes. But I couldn't hurt her feelings — she was much too kind for that. I waved briefly and ran uphill to catch Joanna and Brock. I always seemed to be trailing around after a small child or a dog. One day things would be different, and I'd be free to please myself.

Catching Joanna up, the two of us chased Brock along the dry woodland path which ran close to the river all the way to the house, muddy and squelchy sometimes, but now beaten firm by feet and dried by wind and sunshine.

I was bursting with curiosity and apprehension about my photos. I had the vaguest shadowy memory of taking them, but hardly dared to guess what they might show me. I'd definitely used up several shots before I'd taken the ones of Jonathan in his dinghy. Could I have taken photos in a dream? They might be blank, or they might provide the answer to what had really happened to me after I fell off the gate. I couldn't wait to get home, and Joanna and I burst out of the wood into the full sunlight and ran down the slope to the house. The door at the front was open, the packet of films on the table, unopened. I picked it up and turned it over in my hands, prolonging the suspense. Would it be a complete disappointment, or a wonderful surprise?

"Let's see, let's see!" Joanna was fidgeting by my side, waiting for me to open the envelope. But

I preferred to open it on my own.

"You can see them later. I'm going to look at them first," I said firmly, and took them into the bedroom, closing the door behind me. I stood with my back against it, and slowly opened the packet of prints. The first ones that I took out were bright and glossy — Jonathan in his red-sailed boat on a glittering river, backed by dark woods and a pale sky. He'd like them, but they weren't what I wanted to see. Two blank ones then, totally dark. I held my breath as I turned to the final bunch. The first few fluttered to the floor. There before my eyes was a blurred but unmistakeable picture of Black Magic.

The background was indistinct and shadowed, but the horse was there for anyone to see, and looking straight at me. There was no doubt about it. It wasn't a trick of the light. I thumbed eagerly through the remaining few — all dark and woolly, but it didn't matter. I had one, and that was enough.

A small piece of paper had been slipped in amongst the pictures. The film processors thought I should have some "Hints on taking better photographs." I laughed out loud; they couldn't be any better. I'd got one — and one was enough — unmistakable wonderful photo. He was there, or at least he had been! This was proof, I needed nothing else. It hadn't been a dream — I would go and claim him back. Nobody would keep me from him now.

NINE
Confusion

I started towards the kitchen with a rush, intending to show the photos to Mum and Joanna. I could tell them everything now, show them the perfect horse, even take them to see him! Then a small whisper of doubt crept in as I recalled the wizened man. Suppose he was there again? But he couldn't be. I'd imagined or dreamed him. I was so confused that I couldn't analyse what I'd dreamed and what was real. I only knew that cameras don't lie, and Black Magic was as real as Lorna.

I banged into Jonathan in the hall. "For heaven's sake, Becky, look where you're going, you great elephant!" And seeing the photo in my hand: "What have you got there? Your photos? Let's see," and he snatched the precious snap away.

"I can't make it out, it's too dark in here." He

took it into his room and I watched it jealously as he turned it up and down and sideways.

"Where are the rest of them? This one's no good. I thought you took some of me sailing."

"I did. They're all right, but that's the best one." He passed it back to me. "No, you've made a mistake — there's nothing on this that I can see. It's just a blur. Can I see the others?" He went next door and I heard him picking them up off the floor where I had dropped them.

"What on earth have you left them here for?" he called. "Oh good, there are some ace ones here of the boat. Pity the rest are so awful — no good at all. Can I have these?"

I went in to him: "Yes, of course. I took them for you. I only want this one — it's perfect." He stared at me: "But there's nothing on it, is there? What was it supposed to be, if there was anything to see?"

"Don't keep saying there's nothing there!" I was beginning to get annoyed. "It's perfectly clear — can't you see properly, or something?" I turned away sharply and left him shrugging his shoulders and muttering. But it would have been too much to expect him to understand; he didn't know anything about horses.

My lunch was a hurried affair. In fact I wouldn't have eaten anything if Mum hadn't insisted.

"Sit down for a minute, Becky. You're always

off somewhere. I never see you. Stop fidgeting and tell me what you want to do for the rest of the holidays now that the riding's finished."

"It's not finished," I told her, and waved my photo at her. "Look — what do you think of him?"

She took the picture and held it all ways, and up to the light, then looked at me blankly. "What's it supposed to be? I can't see anything except some shadows. Show me the rest, perhaps they're better. You must have muddled them up — there's nothing on that one." She dropped it into the waste bin, but I snatched it out quickly.

"Mum! I want that!" I looked at it again — he looked better than ever. I could hear the clatter of his hooves and see his glossy mane and tail shaking in the sunlight. Whatever was the matter with everyone else that they couldn't see what was obvious?

"I don't understand you," I said to Mum. "It's a wonderful picture of a perfect horse, and I'm going to ride him every day."

"Becky, I really do think that fall affected you. You could still be a bit concussed. I thought you were better but now I'm not so sure. When Dad gets home I think we ought to take you to the surgery. You can't go on like this — perhaps you damaged your eyesight." I laughed, saying, "I've never felt better in my life! See you later, Mum." I pulled on my wellingtons and left in a hurry before she could stop me. I heard her calling various warnings as I went: "Be careful ... don't do any- thing ... not too far ... home in time for ... " For once I ignored everything, and was soon climbing the steep path which would eventually bring me out at the top of the hill. Then I'd head through the familiar lanes to the old barn. I knew he'd be waiting for me and that once again life would be perfect, and the bonds of time would no longer exist for us.

A furry missile streaked past me into the field — Brock had refused to be left behind. I considered taking him home, but quickly decided not to. After all, he had a right to be with us, having shared in our first idyllic time together: Black Magic and I, always with the terrier close by our heels, always our silent companion.

But now he was anything but silent, yapping in his most irritating way, ahead of me, already in the lane. I ran, still puffing from climbing up the steep path, to see what was the reason for all the noise. Up the road was a small figure, trotting purposefully towards me. Brock ran up to it, still barking, but friendly now, tail vibrating from side to side, and his furry body bending nearly double in welcome. Then I could see it was Sam, panting and flushed. He slowed down at the sight of me, and I could tell he was too weary even to wave.

"Becky!" he called when we were within shouting

distance of each other. "She's gone, Becky! She's gone!" He collapsed in a heap at the side of the road as I came up to him.

"Who's gone, Sam? Emma? Gone where?" I wondered where in the world Emma could have gone to, unable to walk with her plastered leg. Then I looked at him closer, in alarm — he did seem frantic. I knew that some people said someone had "gone" when they meant . . . died. No, surely not! Emma hadn't been *ill*. It was only a broken leg. Perhaps she'd had a fall — down the stairs, maybe, from top to bottom. I could picture the scene — Emma lying crumpled and still at the bottom of their steep stairs. I'd never felt safe on those open treads, with nothing to hold on to on one side, and they were bare polished wood, very slippery. My imagination had run away with me, but I stopped it before it went any further. It was frightening the way I could invent things.

"Sam! *Please!* Tell me what's happened!"

"Not Emma. Mum . . ."

"Your Mum? Gone? Gone where? She'll be back, don't worry." I tried to sound reassuring; more than I felt. But I'd interrupted him. He caught his breath and started again; "Not Mum, no . . . Mum said you should be told . . ." He stopped for another gulp of air.

I was getting impatient: "Told what, for goodness sake?"

"Mum said you should be told that Lorna's gone, stolen, vanished, in broad daylight, nobody knows where or who, Mum's really in a state, and she wants you to look for her," he gabbled without taking a breath.

"So your Mum sent you to fetch me?"

"No, she didn't. They don't know where I am, but I thought you'd know what to do. They don't care about Lorna, but the people who're buying her are coming tomorrow, and Dad was furious that she'd disappeared because he'll have to give the cheque back. And Emma was mad because she thought she wouldn't get her new bike, and Adam was yelling because Mum was shouting, so I just ran off and came down here."

"You did the best thing." I felt really sorry for Sam, living in such a madhouse. "Come on, I'm going your way. We'll decide what to do on the way there. I was really worried when you said someone had 'gone'. I thought something dreadful had happened."

"What do you mean? Isn't this dreadful enough?"

"It couldn't be much worse, could it? Poor Lorna; I wonder what's become of her."

Strangely, I wasn't too concerned. Some instinct told me that Lorna would be safe, wherever she was. It was a funny feeling that I couldn't have described.

There was no-one about as we hurried back to

Sam's. The field was empty, the stable silent. The little room that they used for tack was cluttered as usual with bales of straw, boots, brushes and buckets. The saddle and bridle were in their usual places, but no pony, just the clinging scent of her and traces of hair where she had rubbed her neck and mane, or flicked her tail, against the rough walls of the stable.

The scene in the house wasn't so peaceful. Through the back door I could see that Brian was on the telephone, his free hand over his left ear, keeping out the noise. He seemed to be shouting. Lucinda was pacing up and down with a crying Adam under her arm. She too seemed to be shouting, presumably at Emma, who was hunched into the window seat, except for her plastered leg, which stretched out stiffly in front of her, making it necessary for her mother to step over it each time she turned and retraced her steps across the kitchen. The huge sheepdog lay under the table, nose buried in its paws, trying to look small and keep out of the way of Lucinda's pacing feet, and two cats sat like frightened statues on the mantle-shelf, their ears twitching this way and that.

"Your Mum looks really mad," I said to Sam, holding his arm. No-one inside had noticed us. "I think we'd better stay out of the way. And Emma's crying, I think. She must be really upset about Lorna."

"Not about Lorna," Sam answered scornfully. "She doesn't care about her any more. She's just in a mood because she won't get her new bike, that's all. I'm going in, even if you aren't — coming or not?"

With that he banged the door open — they banged everything, that family: doors of all descriptions — front doors, back doors, bathroom doors, car doors, stable doors. Everything had to be banged; windows, dishes, dustbins, hoovers, toys, everything.

I recoiled from the noise inside. Sam's arrival made it worse, because the dog jumped up, almost knocking over the kitchen table, and ran, barking throatily, to the door. Lucinda tripped over Emma's leg and almost dropped the baby, as Emma screamed loudly with pain — real or imagined, I didn't know. Lucinda rounded on Sam: "Don't burst in like that when you can see your father's on the phone! Come in quietly unless you want a slap!" She slapped him anyway, round the side of his head, and his exaggerated yells added to the chaos.

I hung about in the doorway, hoping they wouldn't notice me, and saw Brian slip neatly out of the kitchen when Lucinda's back was turned. She saw me and her voice changed to the friendly briskness that I was used to: "Come in, Becky, for goodness sake! Don't stand about on the doorstep! Perhaps you can be of some use — no-one else can, it seems! Here, take Adam." She thrust him at me, and I held him gingerly, well away from my sweatshirt. This time he did smell awful.

Lucinda swung round: "Brian! Tell Becky about Lorna!" But Brian was missing.

"He's gone out, Mum." Emma spoke for the first time, sniffing a bit and looking out of the window towards the garage. "He's getting into the car—now he's driving out of the garage."

The estate car passed the back door and disappeared. Lucinda made a disgusted noise: "Just like him to vanish when he's wanted," she complained. "Typical! And when I don't want him around, he's always under my feet, getting in the way, like the rest of you!" She stamped away into the dining room, slamming the door, and suddenly everything was quiet. Emma stopped sniffing, Sam stopped yelling, the dog lay down again under the table, and the cats began to wash themselves on their high perch. I looked down at Adam: he was sucking his thumb and looking up at me sleepily. His eyes were almost closed. I breathed a sigh of relief. Now I could think.

But not for long. I had forgotten Brock, outside on his own. I actually had my mouth open, ready to say to Emma, "Now, let's get this straight . . ."

But I hadn't uttered a syllable before a frantic high-pitched barking erupted from outside, and all eyes swivelled towards the window. From beneath the table, the sheepdog leapt at the door and stood with his nose against the glass, barking deeply. The cats vanished from the mantlepiece. Like two streaks of lightning they totally disappeared. The only calm object was Emma, whose expression was bored. She'd become a complete zombie. I despaired of her ever moving again.

The cause of all the commotion was the arrival of a perfectly harmless-looking policeman. Brock, one normal-sized Jack Russell, with an oversized voice and very large teeth, had managed to pin him to the wall. It was hardly surprising that the policeman's face was red and that he looked helpless, as well as harmless.

Sam came to the rescue, and as I opened the kitchen door carefully, holding the sheepdog back, Sam cornered Brock and tied him up in the stable yard, before the dog decided to nip the policeman's ankles. Lucinda reappeared and with one bellow quietened the sheepdog, who retreated under the table with his tail down. I felt like doing the same, and tried to melt into the background with the miraculously sleeping baby.

"You still here, Becky?" Lucinda called to me from the doorway. "For goodness sake put that child down. It's bad for him to be carried about all day. Dump him in his pram."

"I think he needs his nappy changing," I told her.

"Well, you can do it if you want to be helpful. Emma can tell you where everything is."

She clumped outside to speak to the policeman, who was already looking apprehensive.

I didn't particularly want to change Adam's nappy, and I could see that Emma wouldn't help. She was reading a pop music magazine now, and chewing. She looked up at me, and grinned irritatingly. "Turn on the TV for me first, will you, Becky? I can't quite reach." It was on the kitchen dresser, a new small set that I hadn't seen there before.

"Dad got it for me yesterday. I can watch when I'm in bed. He just carries it upstairs for me — it's great. Then he comes back and carries me up as well!" She laughed as she said this, but I got the picture: poor weedy put-upon Brian staggering up the difficult staircase, being very careful not to knock Emma's bad leg against the wall. No doubt Lucinda stood at the foot of the stairs, shouting instructions to him. No wonder he disappeared as often as he could. Who could blame him?

Emma was looking decidedly smug, reclining in the window seat, still in her fluffy dressing gown and white pyjamas, I noticed. I was suddenly aware of my stained jodhpurs and sweaty sweatshirt.

"Becky! Are you listening? I said, I know I can persuade him to get my bike. And *please* turn on my TV."

Suddenly I was angry, my mind full of doubts

about Lorna. I'd felt she must be safe, but here, where nobody cared whether she lived or died, I began to imagine her with strangers and probably frightened. "No, I won't turn it on!" I snapped at Emma. "It's time you got up off your backside and did something useful. If you hadn't been lying around like this Lorna wouldn't have been stolen!" She stared at me, amazed at the outburst. "But ..." she began.

"But nothing!" I snapped again. "Here, this belongs to you!" And I dumped the soggy baby into her fluffy immaculate white lap, and without staying to see the effect, I bolted out of the kitchen door and ran into the stable yard where Lucinda was talking to the policeman.

Sam was there, swinging on the stable door, making it squeak. He heard my feet on the gravel as I crossed the drive, and turned his head to wink at me and raise his eyebrows. I frowned at him, still cross, and my heart sank as I heard Lucinda's tone:

"That's simply not good enough, officer," she was saying. "I must have some reassurance that a thorough search will be made for this valuable pony."

Sam spluttered, and turned it into a cough, swinging out of reach of his mother's right arm, just to be on the safe side.

"If we searched for every missing animal,

madam," the policeman replied reasonably and apologetically, "we'd be neglecting our other duties. We're always short-handed, you know. I'm very sorry, but ..."

Lucinda interrupted him: "This isn't just a missing animal. It's not like some cow that's wandered away from the farm. I told you, it's an extremely valuable pony. If you can't give me the assurance I want, I shall have to get my husband to speak to your superiors about it."

Sam swung hard on the door, crashing into the stable wall, and fell, rolling into a muddy patch, convulsed with silent laughter. His mother rounded on him:

"What's so funny, may I ask? And do you have to roll in the mud like some savage? You've picked up some disgusting habits since you've been frequenting this stable. Go inside—I'll speak to you later." She turned an accusing eye towards me. "Yes ... disgusting habits. And take off those filthy old clothes!" she shouted after him as he ran away in quite the opposite direction.

The policeman was looking embarrassed, and took a step backwards as Lucinda turned to him again.

"Well?" she demanded, her face red.

The policeman fiddled with his notebook, and took a deep breath. "I'll put in a report. There's nothing more I can do, but I think you should make your mind up that it's very unlikely that you'll see anything more of this pony, valuable or not."

He almost ran to his car, which was parked in the road, and without a backward glance he drove away, leaving Lucinda staring indignantly after him. The crisis had brought out the worst in her, and I wanted to make my escape too.

But she spoke more calmly when the car had vanished: "Well, Becky, that's the end of that. No more riding." And then she brightened up: "There will be the insurance money, of course." I couldn't believe my ears. She looked thoughtfully at the empty stable. "I wonder . . . is it big enough for antiques, do you suppose? I've always wanted a little antique shop. Maybe I could specialise in rustic country objects, and dried flowers and herbs, and corn dollies — that sort of thing. They'd fit in with the character of the place, don't you think? It's quite an idea!"

She obviously didn't expect me to reply, so I didn't. It was too late now to go all the way to the old barn, and somehow I didn't feel in the mood. I just felt sad and depressed. The eagerness and excitement had gone. I collected my crash cap and riding gloves, untied Brock, and quietly left.

I don't think any of them noticed me go.

TEN
Black Magic again

That night I had a vivid dream. Black Magic came alive again, so real and living that when I woke I could smell him and hear him. I buried my face in the pillow, trying to recall every detail and store it in my mind before it faded away, the way dreams do.

Water had been everywhere, waves and spray. We had been swimming in the surf, his strong legs carrying me out into the breakers, his head sometimes vanishing beneath the curling waves, as I clung to his mane, tossed and pulled by the surge of the tide.

I hadn't realised that horses would swim. I couldn't see Lorna enjoying that kind of soaking. She didn't really like riding through a puddle.

We'd both enjoyed ourselves in a wild, mad way, with salty water streaming from my hair and face, down over my clothes and his neck. I wasn't cold. I couldn't say if it was night or day. I was only aware of the plunging horse and the breaking waves, and the sound of the surf on the stones. He hadn't tired. It was I who collapsed at last on his neck and pulled his head round towards the beach.

Reluctantly, it seemed, he headed into the shore, showing off, shaking himself and plunging about in the shallow clear water which hissed up the beach and was then sucked backwards beneath his hooves.

I remember half shutting my eyes with dizziness as the world whirled about me, and in the mistiness I fancied that I could see another shape, another horse, clouded and indistinct, but it could have been Lorna standing there, waiting.

Still dreaming, I slid off Black Magic's streaming back, and tried to lead him to firm ground, but he twisted away from me into the water, and I fell, exhausted. The beach had gone, and the stones were hard and round against my back. Half awake and half asleep still, I felt a soft pony's face touch mine, and knew it was Lorna. Other hooves were ringing on cobblestones, and I knew I was in the old stable yard again.

Then came the inevitable change, from dreaming to waking, and with a feeling of utter disappointment I was suddenly fully awake, listening to rain beating against my window and waves breaking on the stone quay, and the tapping sound of the rose bush which climbed up the outside wall. But the smell of horses was there, and the feeling that they had been with me.

It's said that dreams only last a second or two, but mine had seemed endless. It must have been, to leave such pictures in my mind. I lay in the dark, reliving it so that in the morning I could remember every detail, instead of losing it all in a muddled blur.

I couldn't sleep again after that, though I tried to, hoping that the dream would return, but the more I longed for sleep, the more wide awake I felt. When daylight arrived I was tired and miserable, and could hardly keep my eyes open. Joanna woke in her usual boisterous fashion, and I was more snappy than usual with her. I longed for a room of my own. It was awful sharing with a five-year-old.

After I'd made her cry I relented a bit, and decided to be nicer. "Don't be pathetic," I told her. "I'll take you out later, if you like."

"Where to?" she sniffed, her round face tearful and suspicious. I had been a bit moody with her over the holidays. Soon it would be school again; I must try to make amends. "Wherever you like," I told her.

But I couldn't shake off the dream. The reality of it had wound me up. I felt like a coiled spring, ready to go, to search. I had to visit the old barn to find out if Black Magic was there. But I had to take Joanna with me, because I'd promised, and Mum was getting apprehensive when I kept disappearing on my own.

"I don't like it, Becky," she fussed. "You never know who's around."

"Can we go to the beach, Becky?" Joanna asked. "It's windy and the water'll be rough, and there'll be lots of spray."

"No!" I said sharply, and immediately her face fell. "No, not this time. We'll go there another day. It's too far, we haven't got enough time. I've got to get ready for school later—homework I should have done."

"Homework?" Mum sounded exasperated. "Surely you've done it? You've had loads of time. You really are stupid if you've left it until the last moment. What have you got to do?"

"It's all right, Mum. Not much. Don't fuss."

But for once Mum put her foot down. She was definite: "It's not all right, Becky," she said crossly. "You're not going anywhere until that homework's done. Go and do it now, and then let me see it. You spend far too much time mooning about, fussing over that pony of Emma's, wandering about the countryside on your own, and neglecting the important things that have to be done."

"But Lorna is important. Or she was, until she vanished."

"Well, she's gone now, and there's nothing you can do about it. The police said there wasn't much hope of finding her."

"But they don't know where to look! I must try to find her. She might end up as dog meat if I don't!"

Mum stared at me, exasperated. "Stop being ridiculous! She won't be round these parts any longer. I expect she's hundreds of miles away by now. Be sensible, for heaven's sake. Now, go away and get on with that work, and I don't want to hear or see you until it's finished." She gave me a push in the direction of my room, and all I could do to relieve my feelings was to scowl at Joanna.

Jon was still asleep, his hair spiky on the pillow. It could have been an orang-utang lying there. I felt unreasonably annoyed that he could sleep late and undisturbed. I banged my bedroom door loudly, hoping that it would wake him, and had the satisfaction of hearing his bed creak as he stirred. I looked with disgust at the pile of school books on the floor. The last thing I felt like was settling down to work. Usually I could rattle off an English essay with no trouble at all, but now I didn't want to think about it. All I needed was to get away, with freedom to think and to do what I wanted.

Nobody understood. I was nearly thirteen, almost grown-up (I *hated* the word teenager). I wanted to be left alone, not nagged. I didn't want things organised for me, I wanted to arrange my own life, make my own decisions, go where I pleased, and do what I wanted. I needed privacy, a room of my own. It wasn't much to ask, but I knew I wouldn't get it. The only way I could think my own thoughts was to shut myself in the loo or disappear into the fields or the woods.

I sat dejectedly on the bed, my thoughts anywhere but on my English essay. I couldn't even remember what I was supposed to write about, and couldn't be bothered to search for my homework diary to find out the title we'd been given. All my essays were about horses, anyway, so before the beginning of term I could rattle something off, and add the title later. It didn't seem to matter. My English teacher had given up trying to get me to write about something different. She probably didn't read them anyway.

I glanced at the time — but there was a space where the clock radio had been. So now I couldn't even listen to Radio 2 while I worked, and I knew I'd oversleep every morning without the alarm, and end up running all the way up the hill to catch the school bus. It really did hurt me that I'd given the clock radio away, but that was what I'd intended. I wanted to remember, not forget.

I thought about Lorna. How could anyone have taken her in broad daylight, and why did she go willingly with a stranger? Why had no-one heard or seen anything? But then she was so placid, so friendly, she might have gone with anyone. Then a thought struck me, a strange notion. Were we sure she'd been stolen? Could she just have escaped? Would she have run away on her own? It was out of character, because she'd always seemed so contented, so happy and settled, and she had plenty of attention, first from Emma and then from Sam and me, after Emma broke her leg.

Lorna's stable door was always open into the field, which was hedged all the way round. There were two gates leading out of it, one into the stable yard and the other on to the road. She'd never tried to break out before. I was just dismissing that unlikely theory when I suddenly recalled my dream, and the look on the face of the waiting pony. It was all less crisp and sharp now, but I was sure it was Lorna that I'd seen, patiently waiting while Black Magic and I played and fought with the waves. Waiting for what, though, or who? For me, or for Black Magic? I stood up, suddenly wide awake and supremely confident that I could find her. I knew where she was! She'd gone to find him — and I would find her.

There was no time to tell anyone where I was going, no time for anything except to get to Lorna before she vanished into a world of dreams. I was already there as I climbed through my bedroom window and out into the wind which tugged at my shirt as I began to run swiftly uphill, for once hardly noticing the steepness of the climb. At the top of the wood I almost flew over the old stone stile, and out into the field, where the full force of the wind hit me and slowed me down. Over my head seagulls were wheeling and diving, playing in the gusts, white against a heavy, threatening, dull grey sky. I drove myself on across the damp grass, my feet soaking in thin shoes, shivering with cold or perhaps with apprehension.

Rain was falling by the time I had crossed the field, sharp cold needles which pricked my face, and stung. For a moment I hesitated, cross with myself for rushing out of the house without jacket or boots, and angry with the weather.

Don't be so feeble! I said firmly to myself, and ran on, out into the lane, feet splashing through the puddles and mud. It was a desolate day: steely grey sky, freezing rain, and a penetrating raw gusty wind. My shirt was soaked through and I could feel the wetness on my skin as I ran, drips from my plastered hair running down my neck and shaking off my nose. I prayed I wouldn't meet anyone.

I had to stop at the top of the hill. Running uphill had finished me, and my legs refused to lift my feet off the ground any more. I was too wet to worry where I sat, so I just found a corner of a field where two hedges met, and collapsed, out of the wind, into a soggy heap. For a minute or two I

steamed, breathing hard, just like a horse does
after a gallop, but then the chill gripped me and I
had to make a move. Stiffly, I heaved myself over
the gate back into the lane, and began to trot
downhill, heading for the old barn. I knew she'd
be there. There was no room for doubt. All my
instincts told me I was right.

I was hardly surprised when I sensed some living
thing behind me, and turning my head without
stopping, I saw Brock streaking down the road
towards me. The next instant he had flung himself
at my legs, leaping up and wriggling with delight,
trying to reach my face to lick it between barks. If
I hadn't stopped he would have knocked me over.

He was as wet as I was, dripping with water,
and filthy underneath, but almost grinning with
pleasure and pride at having found me. We went
on together more slowly, and every now and then
he turned his head round to look up and make sure
I was still there. I felt it was a good omen to have
him with me. He knew where we were heading
and thought it was right.

We passed quietly by the ramshackle farmyard,
but not quietly enough, because just as we were
level with the gate, the two farm dogs erupted
from nowhere and flung themselves towards us,
standing up on their hind legs with their heads
through the rails, showing their teeth and filling
the quiet place with noise. I ran then, into the

sheltering track, and Brock had the sense to do the same, after a quick snap and growl. I hoped the disagreeable farmer wouldn't follow us. I wanted to get out of sight down the track before we were seen, but as usual there was no sign of life.

We hurried on between dripping overhanging banks of ferns and primroses. My teeth were chattering, with fright as well as cold. The dogs' barking had stopped, but I didn't look round. Although we were out of sight of the farmyard, I imagined I could hear some shouting behind us. Urgency gripped me again, and I broke into a fast run, desperate to get to the broken-down gate and beyond the spinney before I was caught, either by the farmer or his dogs. I could sense pursuit, and a strong feeling of danger.

At last the spiky old gate came into sight, and thankfully I climbed over it without mishap. Brock slipped through the bottom rails, and we ran and splashed our way across the green field, through the familiar overgrown spinney, and under the dripping elms. I held my breath before squeezing past the old ruined outhouse and emerging into the cobbled yard. It was like coming home after a long time away. I was returning to where I belonged. I knew it could look any way I wanted it to—it could be sunny and warm, whitewashed and swept, well-cared for and smelling of clean straw and polished leather. Or it could be neglected and dirty, with cracked walls and broken cobbles, and a sad empty feeling to it.

I could choose. I could make what I wanted of it. I could be completely selfish, walk into the stable, saddle Black Magic and ride away into the enchantment of endless moors and fields and beckoning hills ... I knew he was waiting, that he'd welcome me. We could go on together for ever ... never return.

But Lorna would be there — dear, placid old pony. And she wasn't mine, and she didn't belong here either. My mind suddenly steadied and I knew that I had to get Lorna away first of all. Then I could come back for Black Magic, just as I'd always intended.

I didn't wait any longer. I stepped out from the shelter of the building, into the yard. The cobbles were wet and slippery beneath my feet. My flimsy cotton indoor shoes had nearly fallen apart, and it was painful to walk on the rounded stones. The building stood gaunt and old, derelict and unkempt, overgrown with grass at its base and ivy up the walls. Across the yard the view was blotted out by the driving rain, and a curtain of mist which blanketed the landscape. But that didn't matter, because the stable door stood open, tied back this time with its orange binder twine, and I heard the wonderful sound of horses stirring restlessly among the straw. I ran unsteadily across the yard with

Brock at my heels, slipping and almost tripping in my stupid shoes.

Lorna was there—I'd never doubted it—in the first stall, tossing her head in greeting, reaching forward to rub her soft nose against me. For a second only I rested my face against hers, but there was no time to lose. It was dim in the stable. Even outside it was like twilight, as if dusk was falling. I knew the end stall was occupied. I would come back for him, I would. But first I had to get Lorna away.

She stood patiently as usual while I found her head collar and buckled it on, and then I led her outside, wishing her hooves didn't make so much noise on the cobbles. But I'd been too slow. I could hear dogs, not far away. For an instant I stood with Lorna, searching for another way to escape from the yard, but it was too late. The dogs were almost on us. I stared in horror at the gap at the end of the barn where they would soon burst through, snarling and ready to leap.

But I had forgotten Brock. Jack Russells are well known for their courage. Some people call it aggression, but I like to think they are brave, and protective of their owners. As the dogs hurled themselves howling into the yard, Lorna backed away in fright, rearing and tugging at the lead rope. At the same time Brock flung himself towards the dogs, bringing them sharply to a standstill, and for a moment his warning barking kept them at bay. They faced each other, the two black and white farm dogs eyeing the terrier warily, their heads down, eyes fixed and waiting for his next move. He stood his ground, not ten feet from them, legs firmly planted, his lips lifted to show strong teeth which could rip and tear. The fur on his back stood up, his ears were laid back; he looked ready for a fight to the death. A low menacing growl came from his throat, and he took a pace forward.

Both farm dogs jumped together, not exactly at him, but sideways, as if tempting him to go for one of them. Which he did. He chose the larger one, rushing at him with teeth bared, aiming for his throat. The noise was deafening, as the two dogs clung to each other and dragged themselves around the yard, growling and snarling through jaws which were full of fur and flesh.

Lorna and I backed away together, but she was whirling and rearing so much that it was impossible for me to jump up on to her back as I had planned. She jerked desperately at the lead rope, hurting my hand as she pulled. Her eyes were rolling in panic and her head tossed about from side to side as she searched for a way of escape from the noise of the fighting dogs, who were still locked together, and now blood was beginning to appear. I watched horrified as it spattered scarlet on the wet stones, and ran away in tiny streams.

The second dog was circling, snapping eagerly and waiting for a chance to join in. Brock's short legs scrabbled on the cobbles for a foothold, as he clung on and fought with the bigger dog. They rolled over and over, biting and snarling, drenched with rain and streaked with blood and dirt.

As Lorna reared again, I flung the lead rope away and slapped her on her hindquarters, shouting "Go, Lorna, go! Find a way home! Go on!" She shot forward as I hit her as hard as I could with my hand, and cleared a small bramble bush with a terrific and terrified jump, then disappeared into the curtain of mist and rain. I prayed she'd find her way back to her own stable without coming to any harm, but she was on her own now and there was nothing more I could do.

I backed away from the confusion in the yard. All three dogs were now scrapping viciously, snapping and yelping when teeth found soft flesh. Brock was standing up for himself—it was a fight he could be proud of. I hoped and hoped that he would survive. There was something I had to do before I could help him.

Behind me in the stable it was dark and damp. No golden light shone through into the end stall, as it had done once before.

"Black Magic," I whispered, but the noise of the dog fight from the yard was overwhelming, and I couldn't hear my own voice.

"Black Magic!" I shouted, "Where are you?"

The door banged behind me, and as I spun round in panic I saw a huge black shape rearing up almost to the roof, iron hooves glinting in the darkness. In ecstasy I threw myself towards him, reaching upwards for his black mane, but it was out of reach, and the bright metal flashed above me, striking my head and sending me spinning and stunned to the floor.

The last sounds I heard were a distant neigh and the clattering of hooves on the cobblestones . . . and a man's low voice, soothing the horse.

Nothing more.

ELEVEN
Tinker's End

"He's mine! He's mine! Let me have him! He belongs to me!"

Faintly I heard a voice shouting. Miles away. My head hurt. Why did people have to shout? I wished they'd be quiet. I wanted to sleep, to dream.

Suddenly I remembered. I mustn't dream: it would turn into a nightmare. And I opened my eyes. It hurt, the light was too bright, it was too noisy. There were faces above me, looking down, peering at me. Round unfamiliar faces. I shut my eyes tightly again. A stab of pain shot through my head, and I opened them carefully. "Don't move," one of the faces said, the red mouth moving oddly. It wavered above me, shifting from side to side. I felt seasick. Perhaps I was on a boat? But why? And where?

I tried to sit up, but collapsed, and was immediately sick over the side. But the side of what? The
boat? I couldn't hear any waves — just a pounding
in my head. I swallowed and opened my mouth to
call for help, but instead I heard the same cry:
"He's mine! He's mine!"

The faces danced above me: "Don't, don't," one
of them said, the red lips wobbling. "You're safe
now, you'll be all right."

I hoped so. I hurt all over, and I couldn't think.
I was afraid of what I might remember. Where
was I? Who was I? I wanted someone, but I didn't
know who. My brain wouldn't work. I shut my
eyes again, and the round faces vanished, and the
shouting, and in the darkness I stopped worrying
and forgot to remember.

The next time I woke, it was better. I was going
to be all right. I sighed with relief, and felt tears on
my face. I'd thought I was dying before. I still
didn't know where I was. The room was unfamiliar
and dark, cluttered with old-fashioned furniture
and pictures, green-patterned curtains letting in a
sickly light. I moved my head gently and stared at
my reflection in the long mirror of a towering
wardrobe. There was a large white bandage round
my head. It looked like a piece of old sheet. I lay in
a high bed, greenish-faced, on pale pillows, buried
under a flowered eiderdown. I looked different

somehow.

Something else caught my eye. Next to the bed, on a small table, the face of a man was watching me. I stared back. A faded photograph, spotted with age and damp, and set in an old-fashioned silver frame, was turned towards me. A young man stood there, stiff and uncomfortable in a high collar and belted jacket.

No-one I knew ... but I knew the eyes, even in the half light. Deep-set and piercing, they watched me boldly, and I drew back from their stare.

It was a posed picture—his right hand rested awkwardly on the back of an ornate chair, on which sat a tiny girl, dressed in layers of lace, with a bow in her curls.

I looked at him again, deep into his dark eyes— now they were twinkling, triumphantly I thought, mocking me as I lay uselessly in the soft bed.

A voice made me jump—I hadn't heard the door: "Are you feeling better, dear?" Startled, I knocked the frame on to the floor, and heard the crack of breaking glass.

"Oh no ... I've broken it ..."

I sat up quickly, but my visitor was already bending to pick up the pieces. She was quite an old lady, small and grey, dressed in a wrap-around flowered apron over a thick hand-knitted cardigan.

"It doesn't matter. We can easily replace the glass." She didn't sound cross. When she drew the

curtains back, letting some light into the dingy
room, she passed me the photo: "Look, the photograph's not damaged— that's all that matters."

I held it warily. Without the protecting glass, he
looked more familiar.

"Who is it?" I asked.

"It's me. Can't you tell? No, I suppose you
can't. It was a long time ago . . ."

"But, who is *he*?" I tried again. "And I'm sorry,
but who are you, and where am I?" I felt totally
confused, and a bit scared, almost as if I'd been
kidnapped. My head throbbed alarmingly under
the makeshift bandage.

"You're at the farm now, Tinker's End. Don't
you remember? You had an accident at the old
barn. The dogs sniffed you out, and my boy Perce
found you lying in the old stables. Your little dog
was having a bit of a scrap with our two."

A bit of a scrap, I thought—what an under-
statement!

"Brock!" I said aloud; "Where is he? Is he safe?"
I felt afraid for him when I remembered the ferocity
of the fight.

"He ran off when Perce arrived on the scene,
frightened of Perce's stick, I'll be bound! Your
pony had gone too, I'm afraid. Perce had shut her
up when he found her wandering yesterday—of
course he didn't know who she belonged to. Were
you looking for her? You shouldn't have been

there, you know. Nobody goes there. It's not safe: the stables haven't been used for years, not since Father went."

She sat down on the bed. "That's his picture you're holding. This was his room. I keep it just as he left it. He's been gone fifty years now."

I stared at her in astonishment: "Fifty years? Fifty years since he was here, and you've kept the room just the same? But why?"

The old lady smiled. "I like to feel that he's still here, that he hasn't left us. I think he'd like that. He'd like things to stay the same as they were."

I began to feel uncomfortable, lying back on Father's mattress, on his pillows, and I swung myself carefully out of the high bed. I did look different: the wardrobe mirror showed me draped in a spotless white nightgown with long sleeves and a high neck. It didn't look like me at all. I matched the room; fifty years ago or more I would have fitted in there. But it wasn't me, I wasn't really part of it. I put the photo back on the little lace-covered bedside table and asked, "Your Father—did he ever go to the old barn?"

"Why, bless you, of course! Every day. It was filled with horses. They were his life. He bred them, you see, from his stallion. Look, that's his picture." She nodded towards the wall over the head of the bed. I don't know why I hadn't seen it before—another photograph in a cheap gilt frame.

A black horse, standing alert and proud, shining and strong with health and vigour, unmistakeably Black Magic.

I couldn't take my eyes off it.

"Yes, that's him," the old lady was saying. "The old Black Devil, Father used to call him, and what a devil he was. It was only Father who could handle him at all. There was so much fire in him, no-one could ever ride him but Father. They had some wild times together when Father was young and strong."

I laughed. "Yes, yes, I bet they did! He was wonderful!" Immediately I'd said it I looked at her, but she didn't seem to have noticed anything.

"He was indeed, a horse in a million." Her voice changed, softened and almost broke, as if with tears. "Theirs was a strange and tragic end."

"End? Why, what happened? What do you mean? Are they both dead?"

"Of course they're dead. They've been dead fifty years. Drowned, they were. Father took the horse to the sea for a gallop along the sands. He was an old man then, remember. The horse too, a real old fellow, otherwise it wouldn't have happened the way it did."

"What did happen?" I knew already, but I had to ask.

"The old Devil plunged in and began to swim with Father still on his back, right out in the deep water. Father couldn't turn him, he tried all he knew, but the old horse had it in his mind to swim until he couldn't swim any longer, and take Father with him, too. So Father slid off and tried to get back to the shore, leading the horse, but Father was a poor swimmer and never reached the land, and nor did the horse." She paused. "They weren't found, either of them. They were seen galloping on the sand, and then swimming out. But the seas were rough, and they were never seen again."

She looked at me: "Can you imagine the scene — what it must have been like for him?"

"Oh yes." My brain was whirling, full of questions with no answers.

The old lady was talking on: "For a long time we didn't believe he was dead. We waited and waited for him to return. I suppose I'm still waiting." She laughed self-consciously; "That's why the room's still the same, you see."

"Yes, I do see," I told her. "I do see that you can wait and wait for someone. Even if they never come back, you don't stop hoping."

She looked at me with surprise, her face old and tired. "No-one else has understood. Everyone thinks I'm crazy, a crazy old woman, even Perce, my own son."

"What about the other horses?" I asked. "What happened to them?"

"Well, there were just a few mares and foals

left — not like it used to be when Father was a young man. They were very restless when the stallion didn't come back. They didn't settle, as I remember. They would have followed him any-where, and they pined for him, waiting, day after day. I couldn't explain it to them, poor things, and they were no use to me, trying to keep this place going without Father, with only my lad to help, and he's been more of a hindrance at times, with that bad temper of his. So the horses had to go — to market in the end. After that the barn was left empty and the stables were never used again. They've stood empty for fifty years — no-one goes there now — falling down, without a horse in them, until Perce found your pony yesterday."

"But she's not my pony. She belongs to my friend. I was looking for her, because we thought she'd been stolen. She vanished from her field yesterday."

"Oh, I think you must be mistaken. I don't think she can have been stolen. Perce found her standing in front of the stable, he said, waiting patiently, as if she was expecting someone."

"Perhaps she was."

"No — she must have broken out of her field and wandered away. She hadn't even a head collar on, and there was no sign of anybody."

"I don't mean that. Perhaps she was waiting for someone, for the black stallion."

The old lady looked at me oddly: "That was fifty years ago, girl. That bang on your head must have turned your brain."

It was only then that I remembered my head. "What happened to me? What hit me? It was as if something fell."

"Something did fall — a beam from over the stable door. It had some old horseshoes nailed to it and one of them must have cut your head when the beam hit you. You were lucky — it could have been a lot worse."

Black Magic's horseshoe! I knew he'd knocked me down. But I'd never believe that he meant to hurt me. I understood now that he couldn't have come with me, that he had to stay with the old man. I looked up at his picture again. I wanted it. It must have shown in my face, because the old lady leaned over the heavy wooden bed-head and lifted it down from its nail on the wall. There was a light patch on the faded flowered wallpaper, where it had hung for so long. She held it out to me: "Here — take it. I don't suppose he'd mind, and I can see it means something to you, though I don't know why it should. It's time this room was changed about and tidied up, anyway. You can't go on living in the past, I suppose, can you?"

"No, it's now that counts. Thank you — I can't thank you enough." I gazed at the photo. Though it was so old, I had to admit that it was a lot better than the snap of him that I'd taken. "I'll treasure this for ever," I told her, "and I'm really sorry for breaking the glass on your Father's photo."

"It doesn't matter, it's time he was put away in a drawer. He was an old rascal, mad for horses and not much else. They did say he took what he wanted if he couldn't get it any other way. Horses — he always wanted more . . ."

I could understand that. Now I had to let go, and stop wanting something I could never have. The dream was over.

Not long afterwards, when I had groped my way down the creaking dark stairs, feeling normal again in my jeans and shirt, warm from drying by the kitchen fire, Dad and Mum and Joanna arrived. I'd never been so pleased to see them before. Their arrival was announced by a storm of barking from the farm dogs, and I ran to the little window that looked over the farmyard expecting to see the dogs savaging whoever was coming to the door. Surprisingly, they were wagging their long tails in a welcoming manner, and letting Joanna pat their heads and stroke them, as Dad and Mum carefully picked their way across the mud-covered yard. In front of them Brock strutted, very pleased with himself, leading the way to the front door. I couldn't believe that the last time I'd seen him, he'd been fighting for his life with those two. What had been a dream and what was reality?

The old lady was peering over my shoulder to see who was coming. I must admit I was relieved. I'd had a funny feeling that I'd stepped back in time, and might not be able to retrace my steps and return to normal.

"Someone's come to get you, by the look of things," she remarked. "I don't know those people, so they must be for you."

"Yes, it's my parents — and my sister and her dog."

"Ah, then it'll be him who's led them to you. Animals have a way of finding out."

The man Perce was sitting at the large table in the middle of the kitchen. He'd nodded to me when I opened the oak door at the bottom of the stairs and stepped into the room, but hadn't spoken. I found it hard to believe that this man, who'd been so unpleasant when he'd found me sunbathing — as he thought — by the gate, had carried me here in his arms, unconscious. I owed him something, so I said gratefully, "Thank you very much for rescuing me. I was looking for my friend's pony. I'm sorry I caused you all that trouble."

"It was the dogs that found you — lying on the floor you were, as still as anything. Gave me a fright, you did. Your terrier would have ripped me to pieces if I hadn't had my stick ... the pony's gone, too. You'll be lucky if you get her back now."

"I let her go. I sent her off, told her to go back home."

"Stupid thing to do, if you ask me! She'll be miles away by now. Waste of time me catching her, wasn't it?"

He turned away to the old black range which filled the chimney alcove, and poked bad-temperedly at the glowing fire. Unshaven, and wearing the same dirty shirt, he didn't look any better than when I'd seen him before. Only the trilby and the sacks were missing. It seemed an age ago that he'd been shouting at me and waving his stick. I felt really sorry for the old lady, having to exist there with him, even if he was her son.

I noticed an old oil lamp on the table, and candles on the mantlepiece. The ceiling was low and black-beamed, the walls a dismal yellowish colour, stained by smoke. There was nothing modern or up-to-date about this dwelling: everything was old and worn, including the people who lived there.

The old lady drew aside a dark heavy curtain which hid the outside door, and kept out the draughts, and opened the door so that I could see daylight and the figures of Mum and Dad and Joanna, with Brock wriggling with pleasure at their feet.

Soon, clutching the precious photograph, and explaining about the bandage, I left the strangeness of the farmhouse and crossed the muddy yard, where ducks and geese and chickens scattered to let us through, and closed behind us as if shutting out the past.

TWELVE
Surprises — and a little magic

They didn't understand, of course. I knew they wouldn't. How could they? After a while I gave up trying to explain.

They went on endlessly about me going away for hours without telling anyone where I was going — out of my bedroom window too! And going to places where I wasn't supposed to be. And being a complete nuisance to people who had better things to do than run about after me. And getting myself knocked on the head so that I had to be taken to the doctor for three stitches. At least they couldn't nag on at me in the surgery. It made a pleasant change — the doctor was very sympathetic and said perhaps I shouldn't go straight back to school if I felt I wanted a few days' rest, just in case I was concussed.

But I did go back on the first day of the summer term. It seemed a better option than staying at home in disgrace looking after Joanna.

Then they found out that I'd given away the clock radio, and there was more trouble. Dad said I had to get it back, but I refused point blank. A gift was a gift, and I'd been free to do what I liked with it.

It was all so unfair! Hadn't I found Lorna for Emma? Just as I hoped, she had found her own way home, and Sam, looking out of the kitchen window, had seen her standing patiently, dripping with rain, in the drive. Lucinda's first reaction was one of dismay. She had already been planning the craft and antique shop that she was going to set up with the insurance money.

Of course the sale had fallen through when the prospective owners had arrived to collect Lorna and found her missing, and Brian had to give the cheque back. But then he had a complete change of heart, and I got quite a surprise when Sam phoned to tell me that Lorna was staying after all. His Dad had said he didn't need the money anyway, and he'd decided he liked seeing Lorna grazing in the field when he looked out of the bedroom window. He thought it was much better than having an arty-crafty shop on his doorstep, with cars parking outside the house and strangers wandering around the garden, knocking on the door wanting to use the loo. Sam said Brian had even said something about buying a horsebox to take him and Lorna to gymkhanas.

Of course Lucinda wasn't too pleased at first, but she got over it when Brian bought her a new wax jacket and a pure silk scarf.

I was really pleased to hear about Lorna, and school wasn't too bad either. I was actually glad to be back, and see my friends, and I handed in the money I'd collected for the sponsored fast, wondering if I'd ever have seen the real Black Magic if I hadn't done the fast and fallen off the gate. It was a funny thought.

If I couldn't have my dream horse, I didn't want one at all, I told myself, and, with a bit more enthusiasm than before, I joined in school activities. Everyone of my age seemed to have a boyfriend, and there was someone in one of the third-year groups who I thought looked really nice . . .

Emma and I compared notes about him, and the boy that she liked, on the way home in the bus. She told me that Brian had bought her the new bike, even though he hadn't got the money for Lorna. It had been very expensive, a racing bike with ten gears, and she made sure that everyone knew, although she couldn't ride it until her leg was out of plaster. She was still making the most of it, having to be helped everywhere, and getting out of lessons she didn't enjoy. It was a pantomime getting her on and off the school bus, and we were always late by the time she had hobbled her way into school on her crutches. Naturally my stitches were nothing compared to her plaster, but at least we were friends again, and we discussed pop music and the programmes we'd seen on TV, and made plans for the summer holidays. We giggled and joked about the teachers, and said unkind things about other people at school, just the same as everyone else did. They all forgot that I had been "horsey" before, and therefore different, and at last I began to enjoy myself again.

Sometimes when the bus was grinding up the steep hill to the crossroads where I got off, I spotted Sam in the lane, riding out on Lorna. He had plenty of time after getting home from the village school, but I told myself I wasn't envious as I waved casually to Emma and the bus driver, and walked slowly home down the other side of the hill. The river stretched away in front of me, a stretch of grey-brown mud at low water, or a sheet of silver when the tide was in, reminding me of summer and sailing.

At that moment my heart usually sank, and I knew that horses would always be my passion. Everything else was pretence.

I longed for the day when I was old enough and had enough money to buy my own horse. It couldn't come too quickly for me.

The weeks went by uneventfully; boringly, if I was honest. And then I got a surprise. Well, we all did. Lorna was in foal! Emma was quite certain; the vet had been out and confirmed it. She said her mother was furious. Lucinda said it would just make more work for her, and once again she wanted to get rid of Lorna. But Brian wouldn't hear of it, as Sam was riding so well and it was keeping him out of mischief, so Lorna was staying.

It never occurred to me to wonder, not until I saw the little wobbling foal for the first time, staggering bravely about on its delicate long legs. It was black! As black as night. Magically black!

I leaned over the stable door, and stared and stared, trying to work it out.

"What do you think of him, Becky?" Sam asked. "What shall we call him?"

Lorna was gently licking the foal, nudging him with her soft nose. The stable was warm and homely, glowing with the soft light from above and the yellow straw underfoot. It was a marvellous sight, and at that moment I knew that somehow the foal would be mine. Emma wasn't the only one who could get round her Dad. Somehow I would persuade him. It was just a case of waiting for the right moment.

Black Magic had gone for ever, and at last I could think about him without pain, as I stared in wonder at his offspring.

"It's Magic," I said softly; "Just like Magic."

"That's it, Becky!" Sam was smiling too. "That's what we'll call him — Magic!"

Lorna lifted her head and her eyes met mine, and I knew that she approved.